DREAMWORK

THE EPIC TALES o
CAPTAI UNDERPA

THE MANIACAL MISCHIEF OF THE MARAUDING MONSTERS

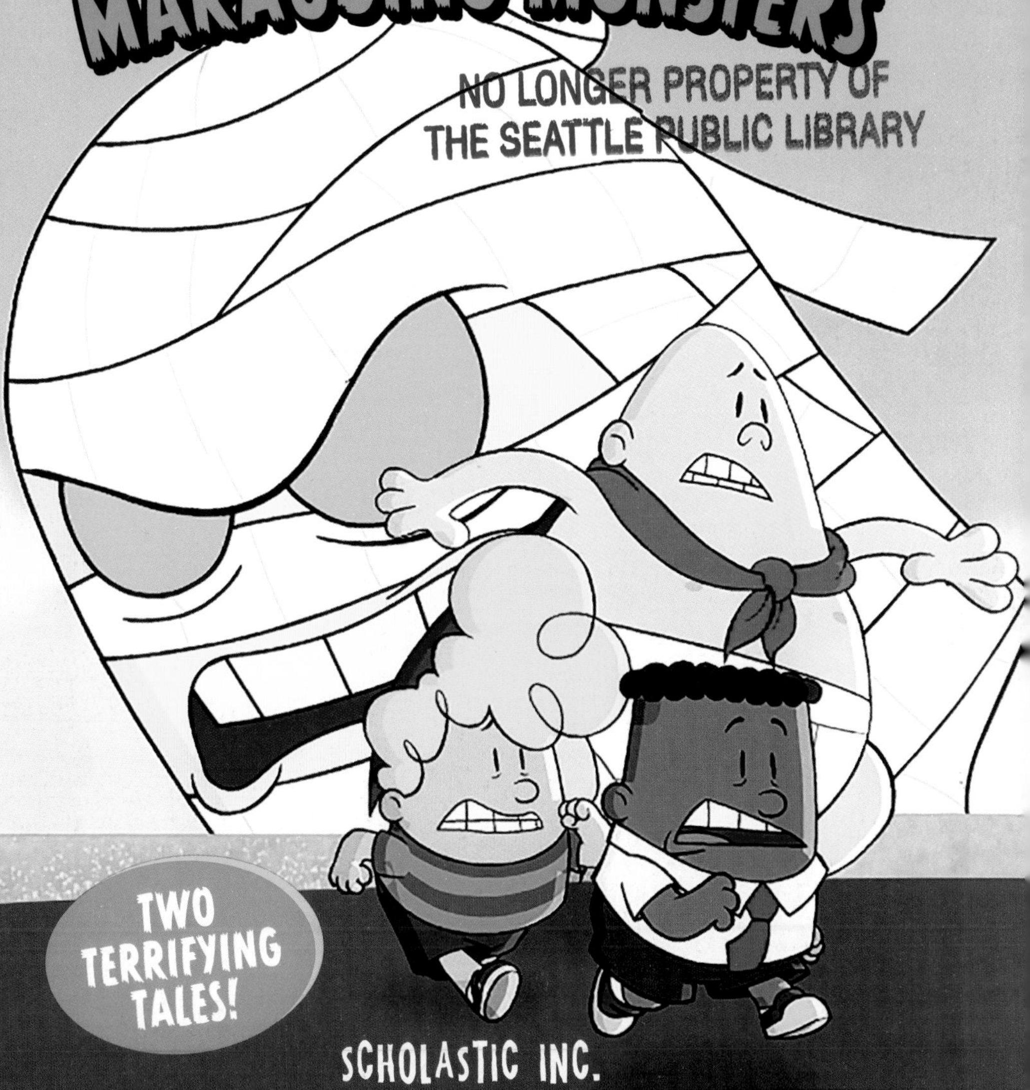

TWO TERRIFYING TALES!

SCHOLASTIC INC.

ISBN 978-1-338-86556-1

10 9 8 7 6 5 4 3 2 1   23 24 25 26 27

Printed in the U.S.A.   40

First printing 2023

Book design by Jessica Rodriguez
Adapted by Meredith Rusu
Stock images © Shutterstock.com

THIS IS GEORGE BEARD AND HAROLD HUTCHINS.

George is the kid on the left with the flat top and waxed mustache. **Harold** is the one on the right with the bad haircut who also has a waxed mustache. Remember that now.

George and Harold have seen a lot of strange things. But nothing compares to the truly terrifying monsters that appear in their most spine-tingling adventures. Creatures so ghoulish, they can make even a superhero need an extra pair of underpants.

Within these pages are tales of two of George and Harold's most harrowingly haunted exploits. They're not for the faint of heart. And they definitely shouldn't be read at night. In the dark. When you're supposed to be sleeping. (Because it's a school night.)

TURN THE PAGE IF YOU DARE . . .

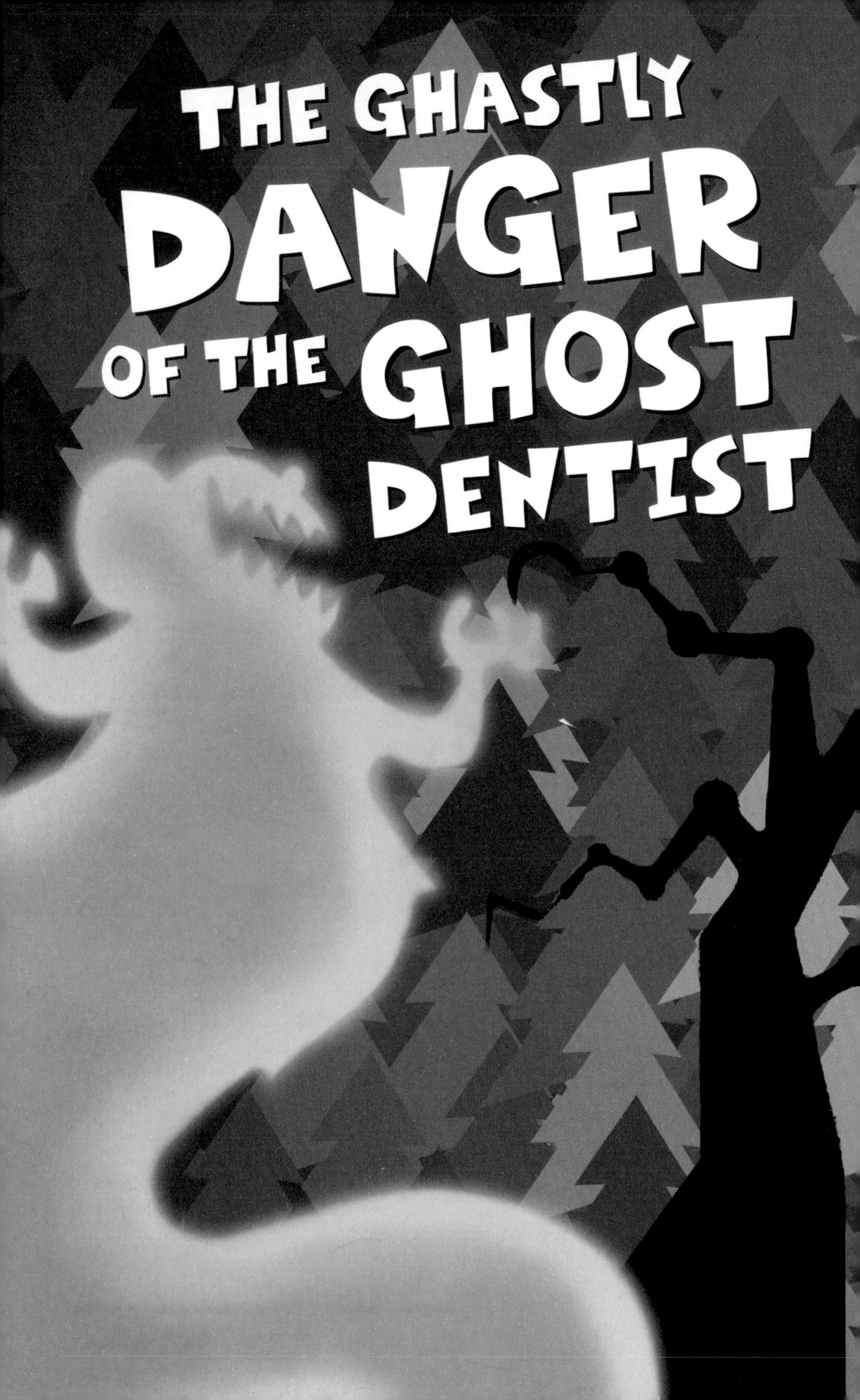
THE GHASTLY
DANGER
OF THE GHOST
DENTIST

CHAPTER 1

TOOTH OR DARE

It was the night of the annual Campfire Story Telling-a-thon at Lake Summer Camp. And George and Harold were planning to tell the creepiest story ever.

Check it out. I have the perfect idea for a spooky story.

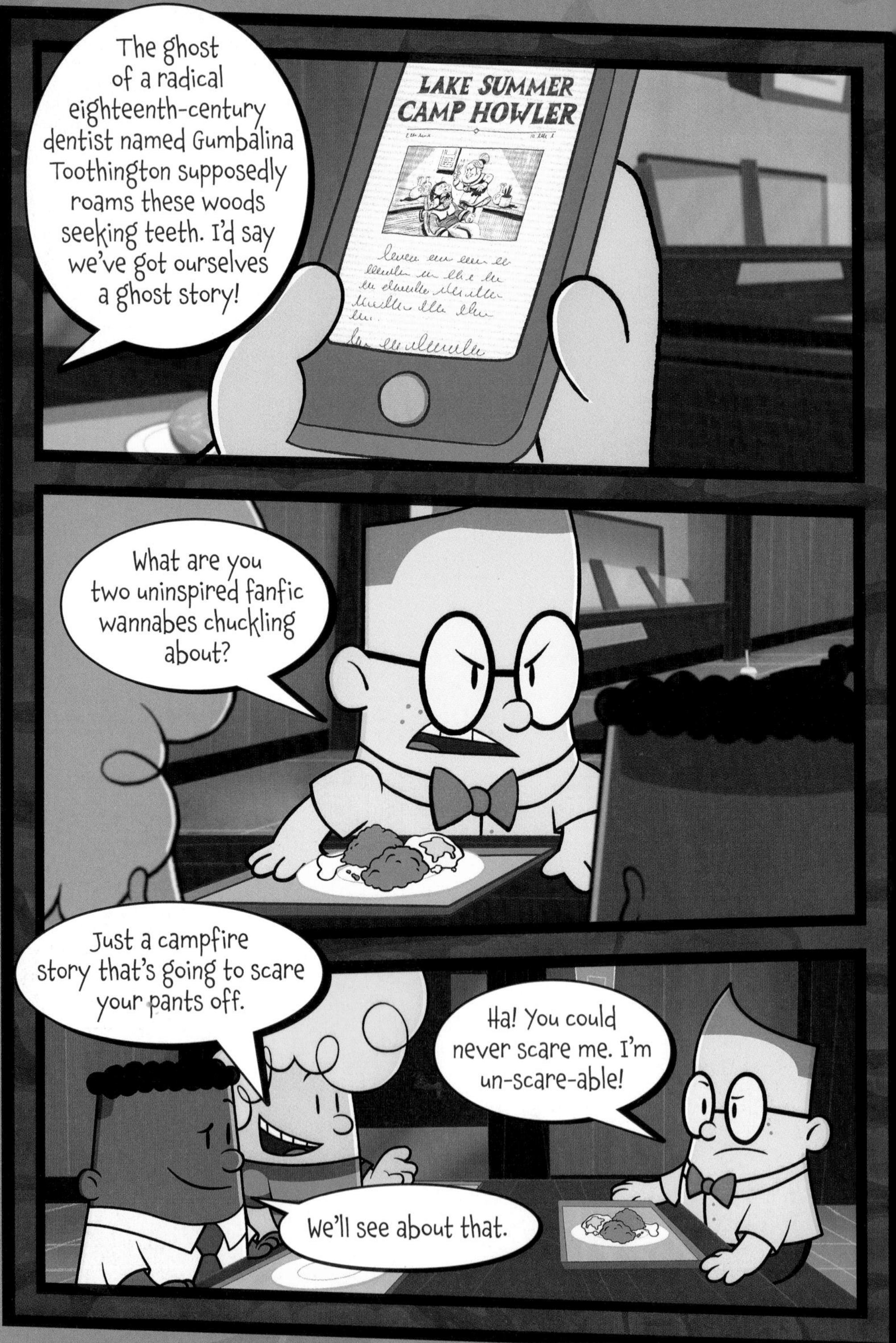
The ghost of a radical eighteenth-century dentist named Gumbalina Toothington supposedly roams these woods seeking teeth. I'd say we've got ourselves a ghost story!
LAKE SUMMER CAMP HOWLER
What are you two uninspired fanfic wannabes chuckling about?
Just a campfire story that's going to scare your pants off.
Ha! You could never scare me. I'm un-scare-able!
We'll see about that.

A SCARE TO REMEMBER

That night, at the campout . . .

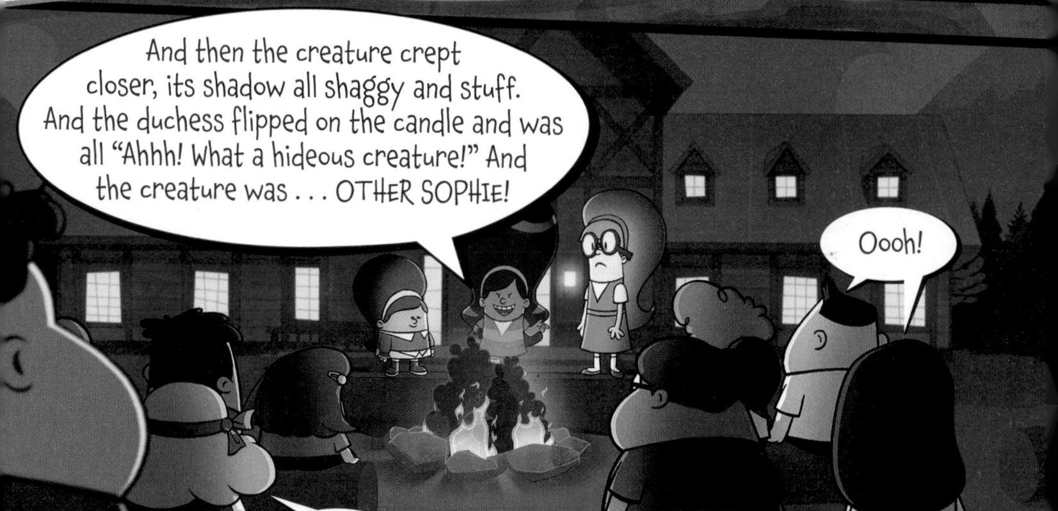
And then the creature crept closer, its shadow all shaggy and stuff. And the duchess flipped on the candle and was all "Ahhh! What a hideous creature!" And the creature was . . . OTHER SOPHIE!
Oooh!
Chills!

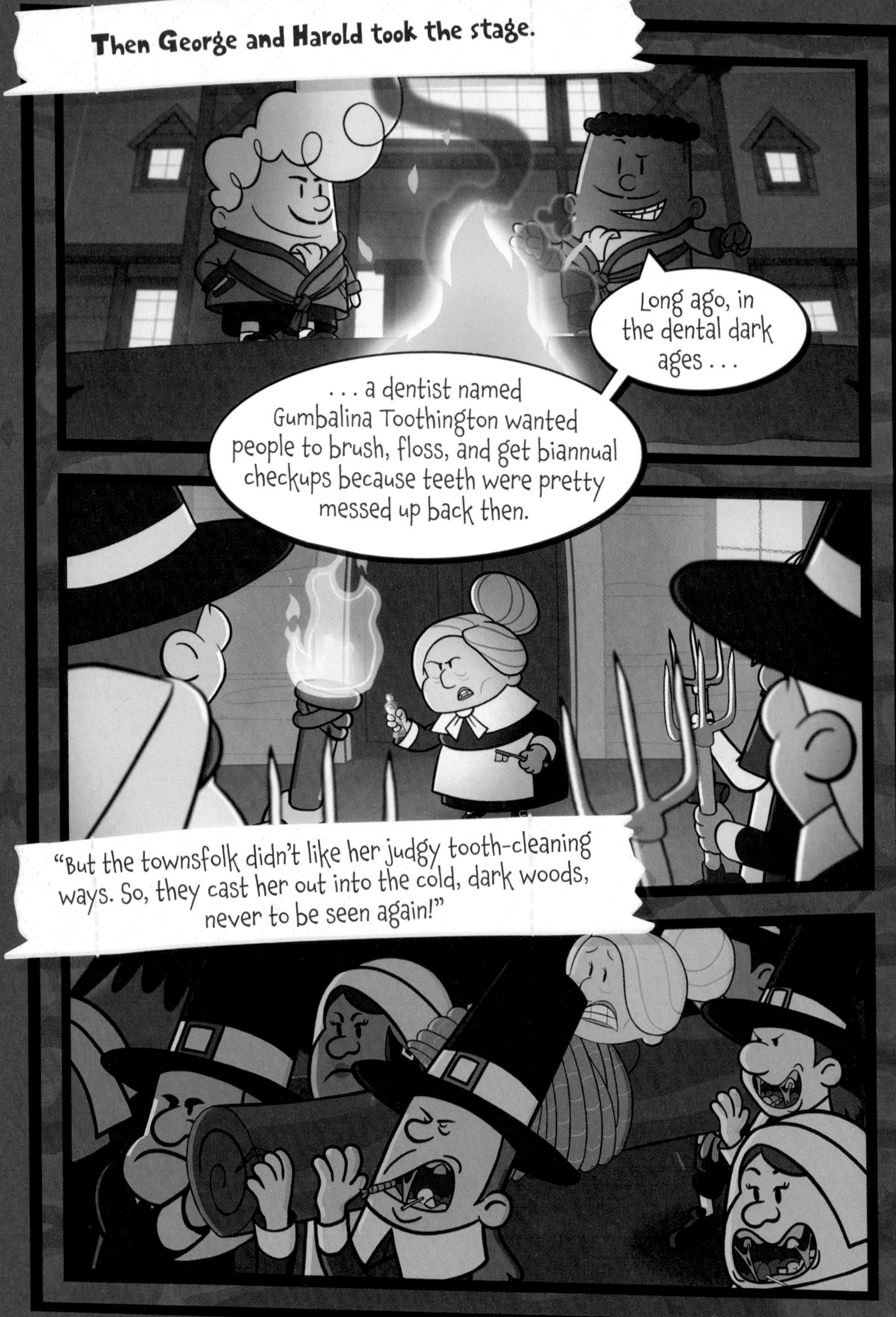
Then George and Harold took the stage.
Long ago, in the dental dark ages . . .
. . . a dentist named Gumbalina Toothington wanted people to brush, floss, and get biannual checkups because teeth were pretty messed up back then.
"But the townsfolk didn't like her judgy tooth-cleaning ways. So, they cast her out into the cold, dark woods, never to be seen again!"

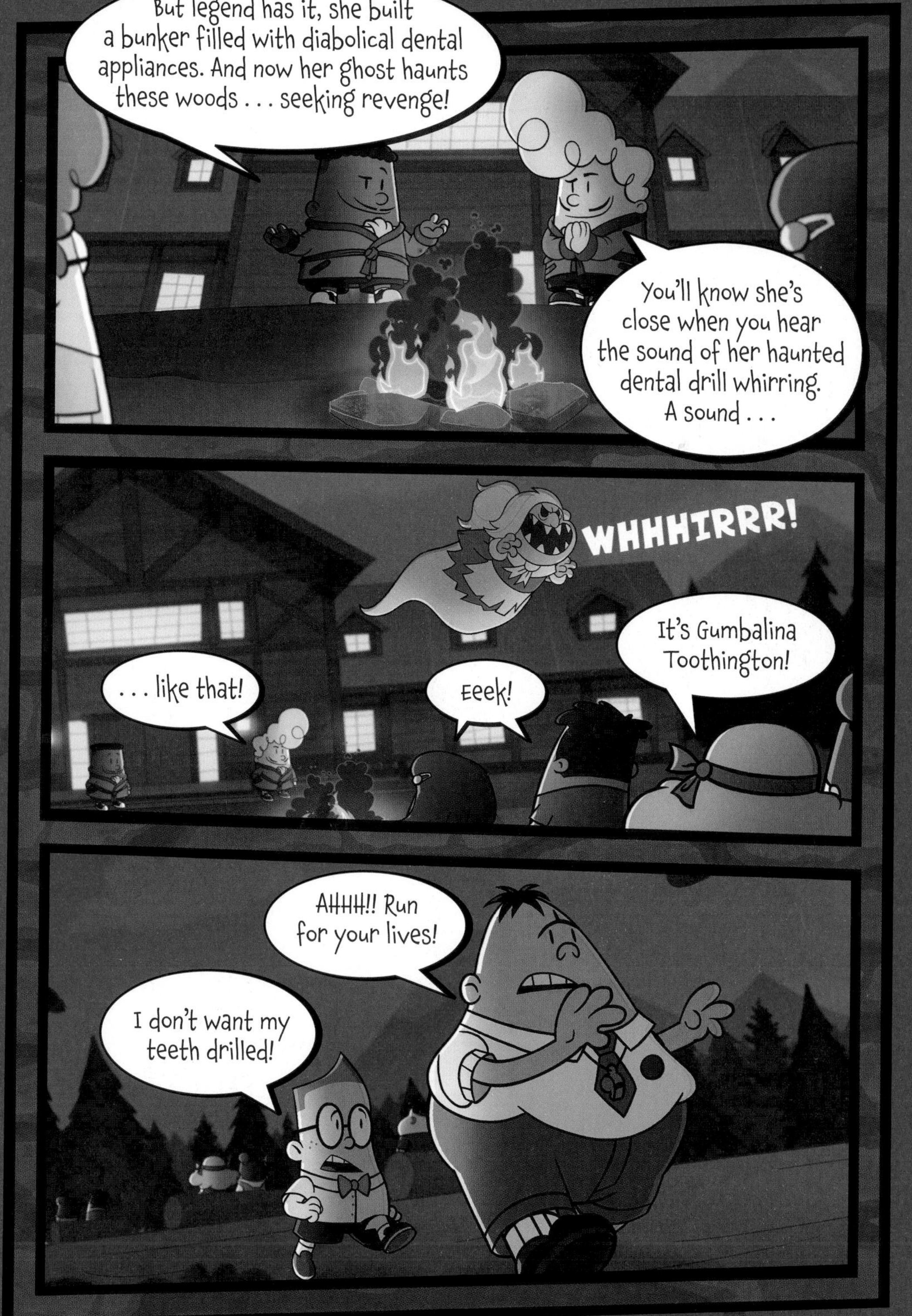
But legend has it, she built a bunker filled with diabolical dental appliances. And now her ghost haunts these woods . . . seeking revenge!
You'll know she's close when you hear the sound of her haunted dental drill whirring. A sound . . .
WHHHIRRR!
. . . like that!
Eeek!
It's Gumbalina Toothington!
AHHH!! Run for your lives!
I don't want my teeth drilled!

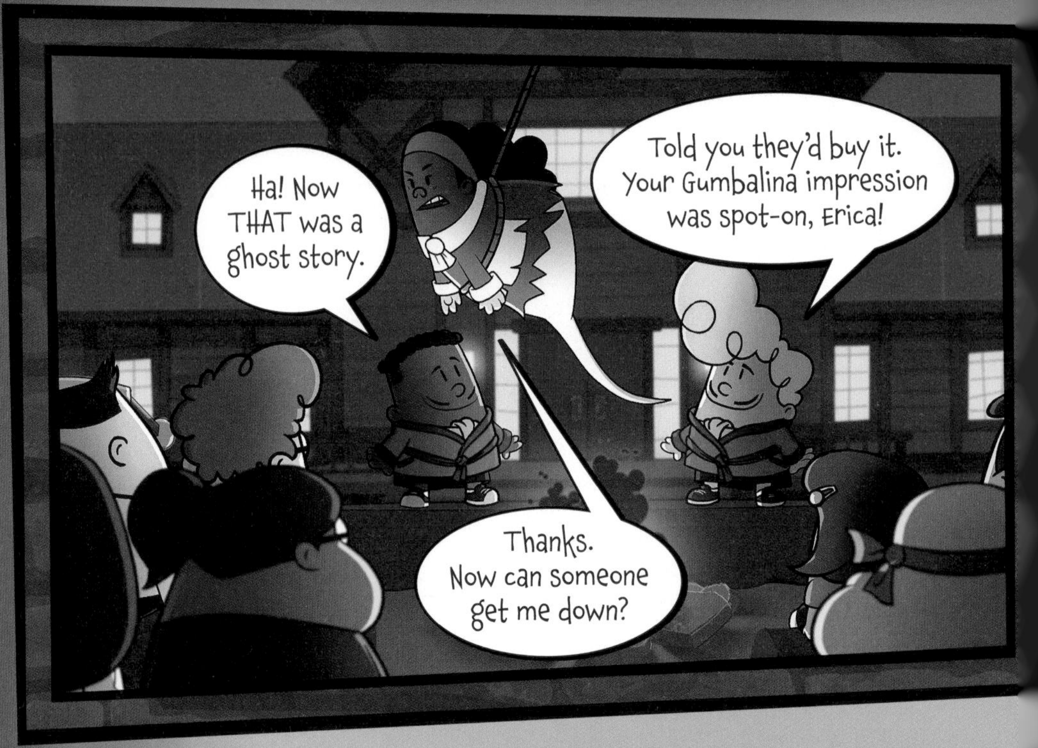
Ha! Now THAT was a ghost story.
Told you they'd buy it. Your Gumbalina impression was spot-on, Erica!
Thanks. Now can someone get me down?

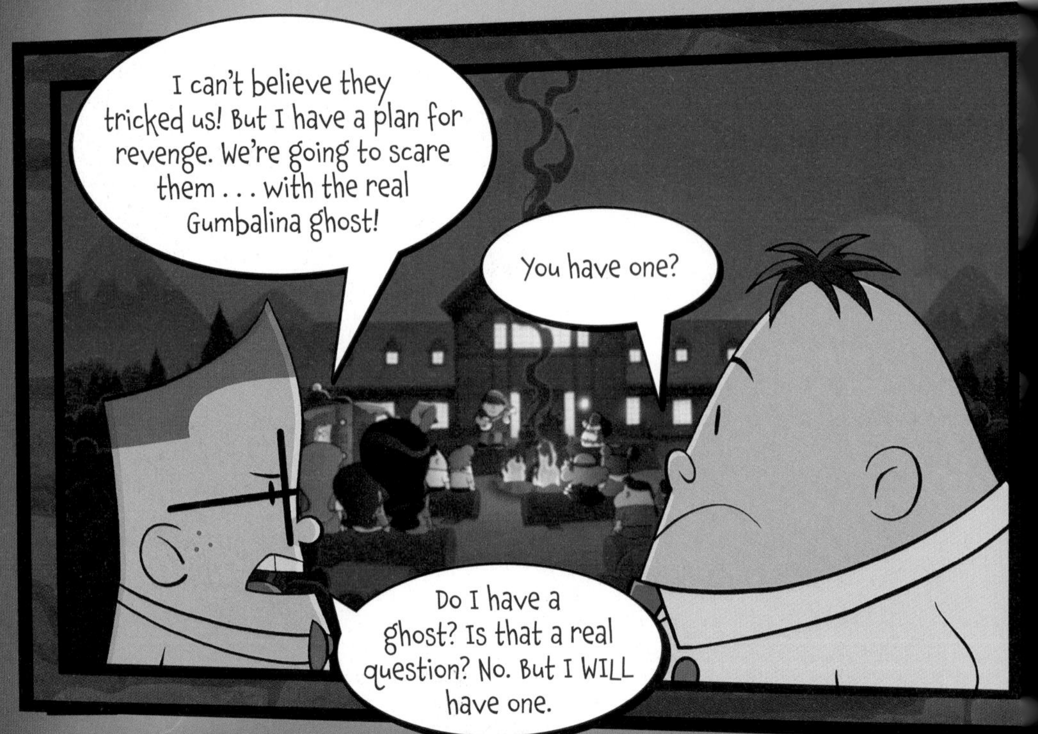
I can't believe they tricked us! But I have a plan for revenge. We're going to scare them . . . with the real Gumbalina ghost!
You have one?
Do I have a ghost? Is that a real question? No. But I WILL have one.

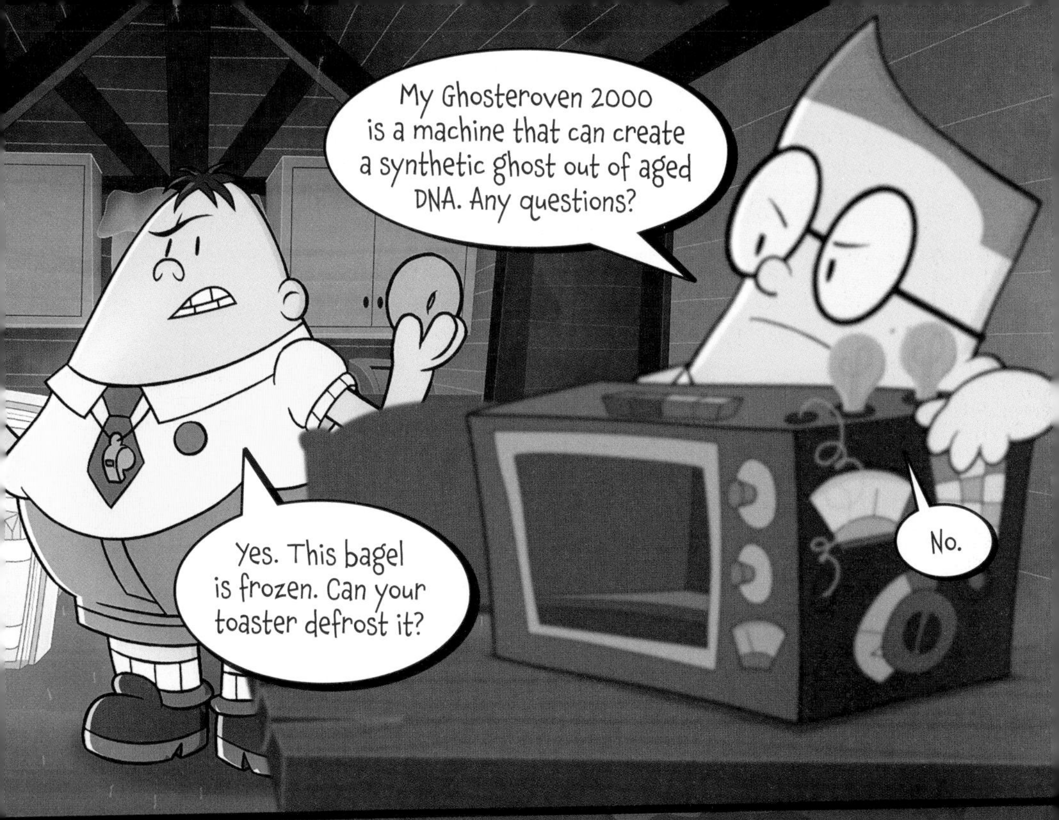
My Ghosteroven 2000 is a machine that can create a synthetic ghost out of aged DNA. Any questions?
Yes. This bagel is frozen. Can your toaster defrost it?
No.

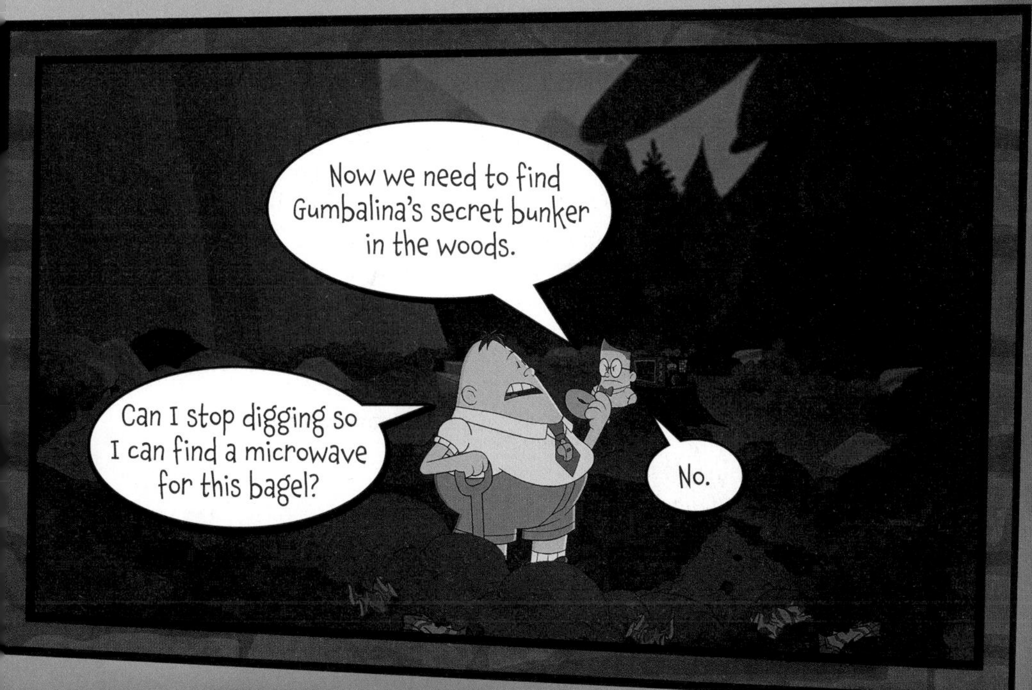
Now we need to find Gumbalina's secret bunker in the woods.
Can I stop digging so I can find a microwave for this bagel?
No.

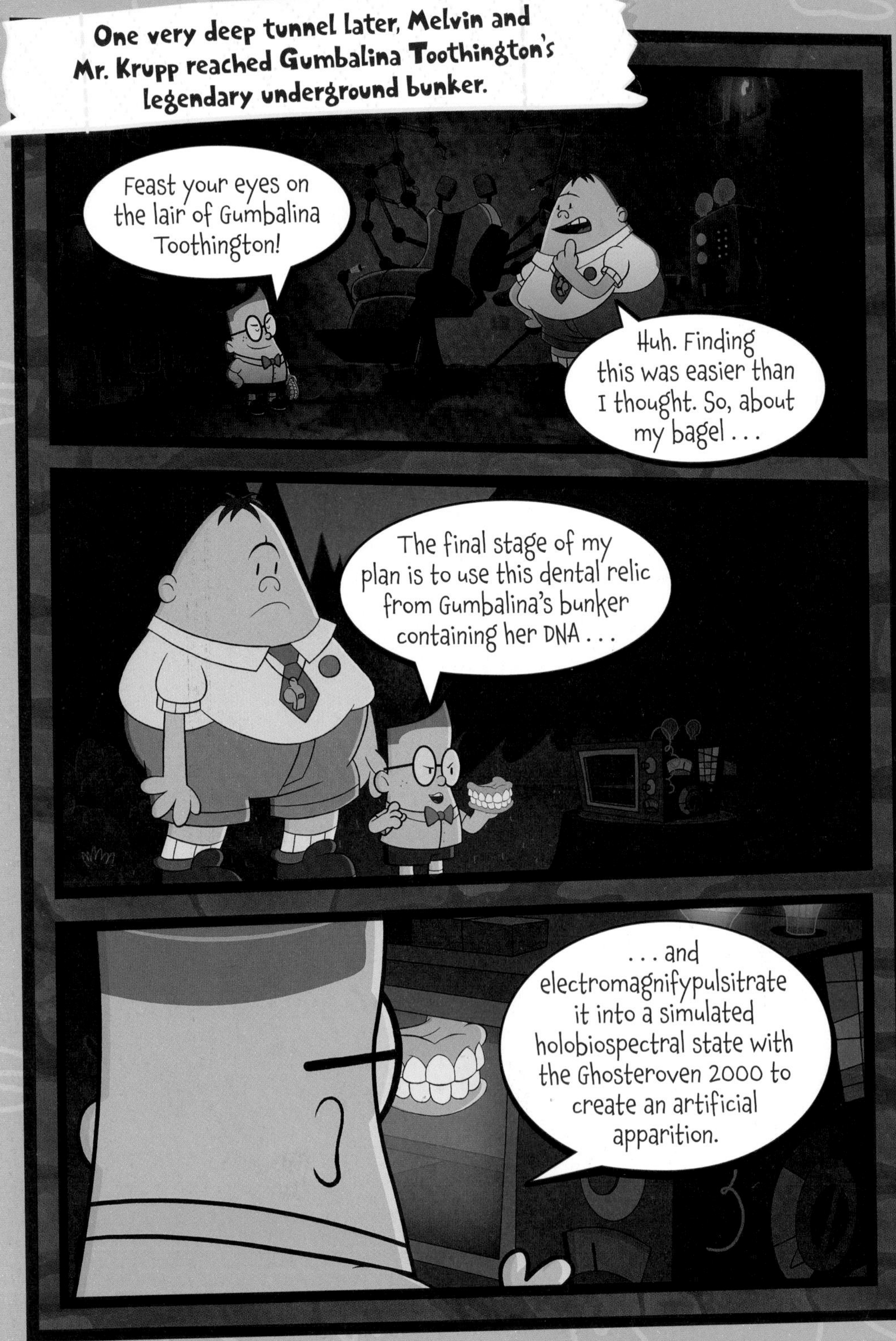
One very deep tunnel later, Melvin and Mr. Krupp reached Gumbalina Toothington's legendary underground bunker.
Feast your eyes on the lair of Gumbalina Toothington!
Huh. Finding this was easier than I thought. So, about my bagel . . .
The final stage of my plan is to use this dental relic from Gumbalina's bunker containing her DNA . . .
. . . and electromagnifypulsitrate it into a simulated holobiospectral state with the Ghosteroven 2000 to create an artificial apparition.

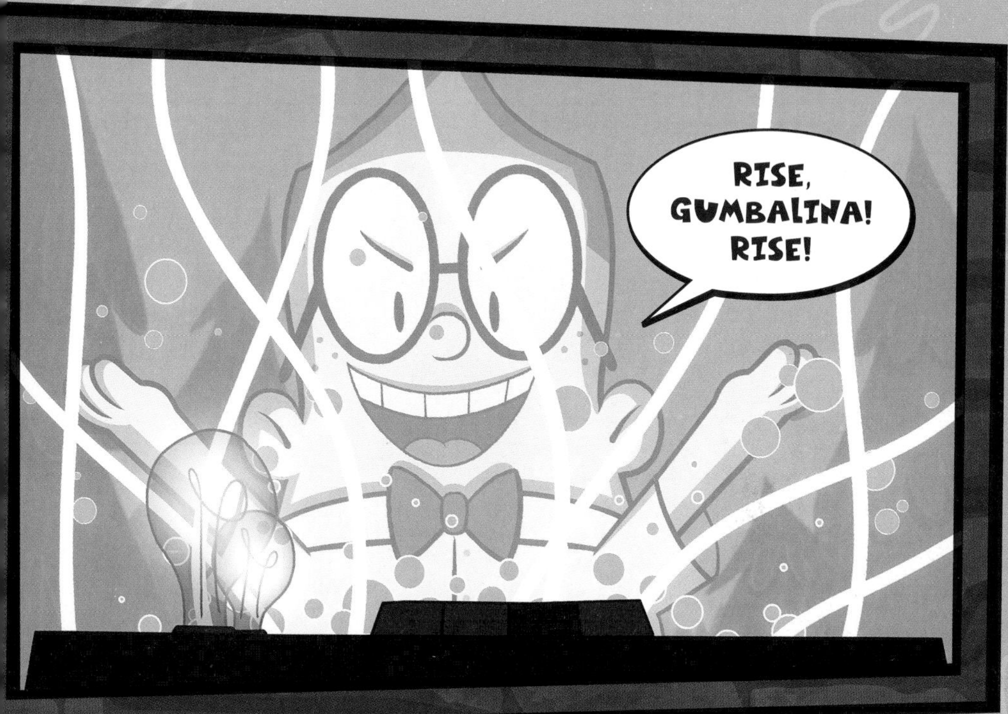
RISE, GUMBALINA! RISE!

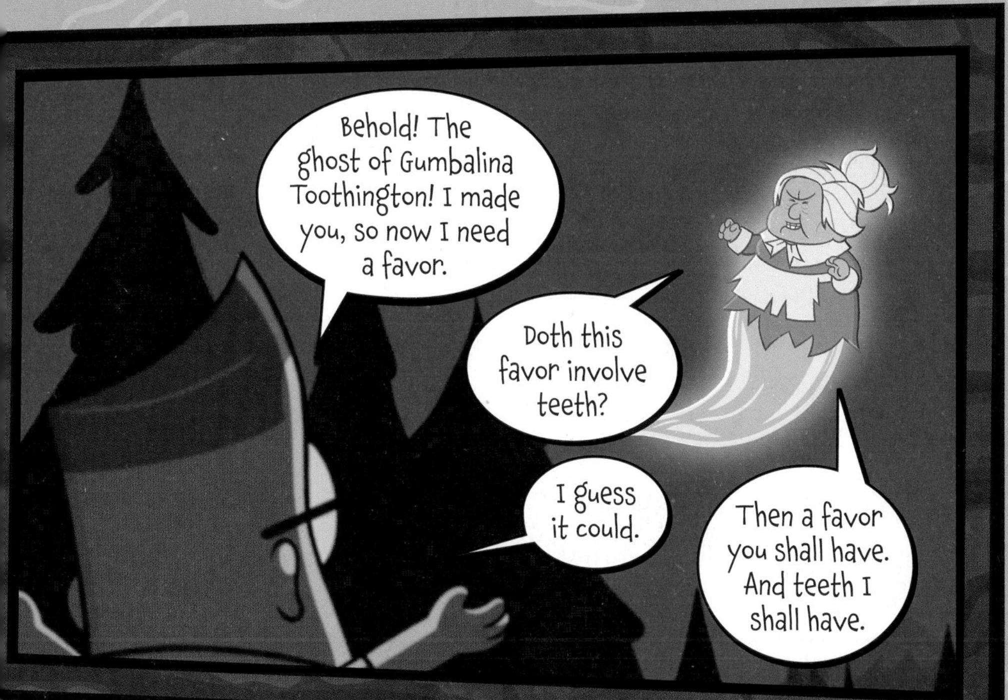
Behold! The ghost of Gumbalina Toothington! I made you, so now I need a favor.
Doth this favor involve teeth?
I guess it could.
Then a favor you shall have. And teeth I shall have.

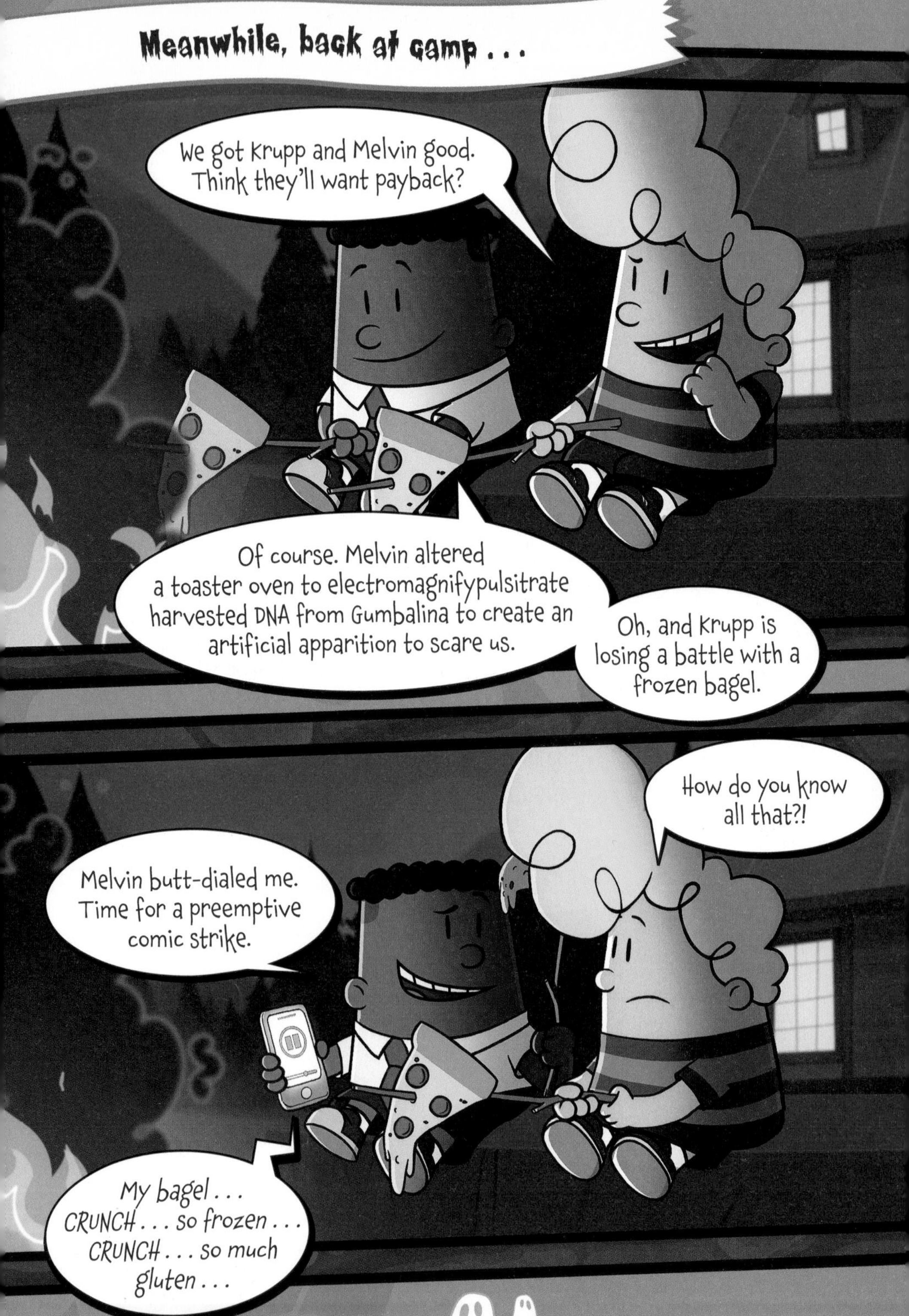
Meanwhile, back at camp . . .
We got Krupp and Melvin good. Think they'll want payback?
Of course. Melvin altered a toaster oven to electromagnifypulsitrate harvested DNA from Gumbalina to create an artificial apparition to scare us.
Oh, and Krupp is losing a battle with a frozen bagel.
How do you know all that?!
Melvin butt-dialed me. Time for a preemptive comic strike.
My bagel . . . CRUNCH . . . so frozen . . . CRUNCH . . . so much gluten . . .

CHAPTER 3

CAPTAIN UNDERPANTS and the GHOST DENTIST

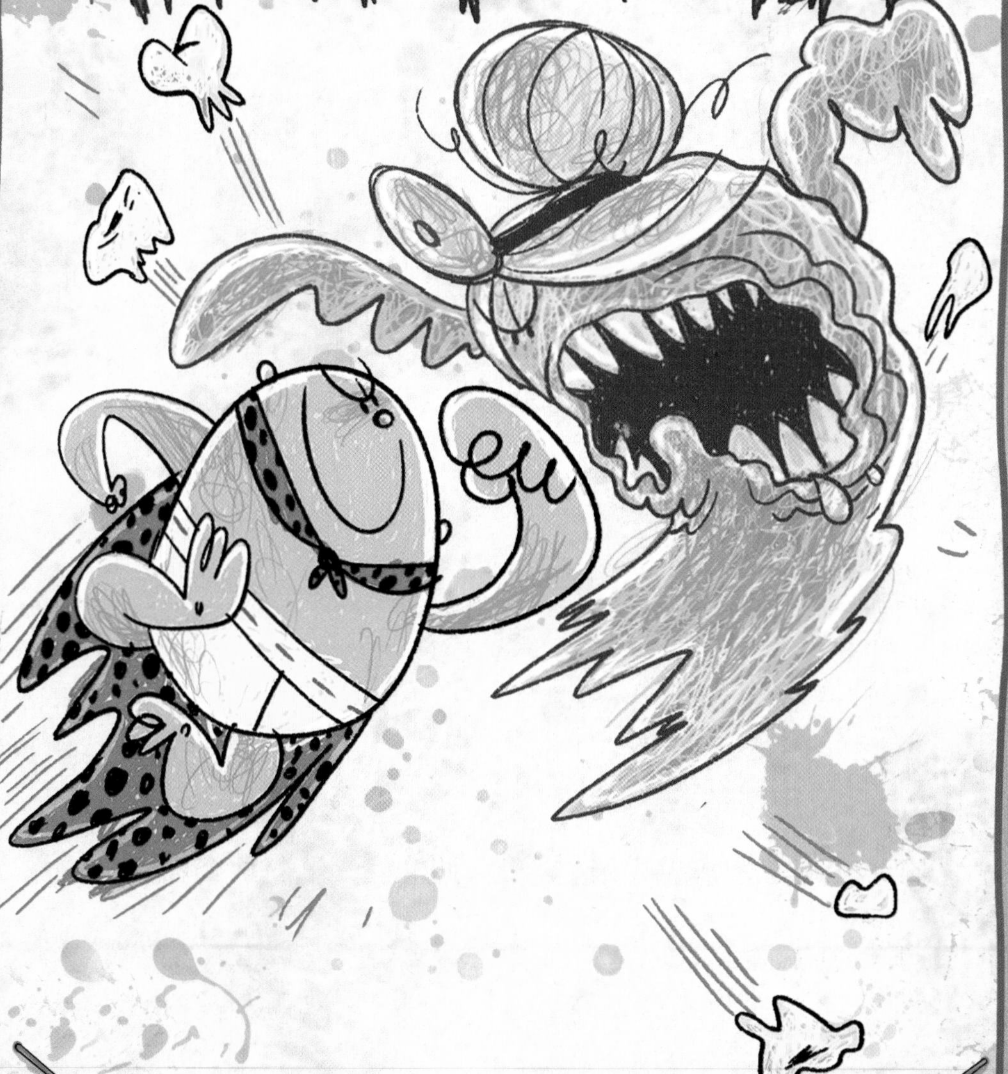

Once, there were these ghost experts named Mr. Mupp and Krelvin.

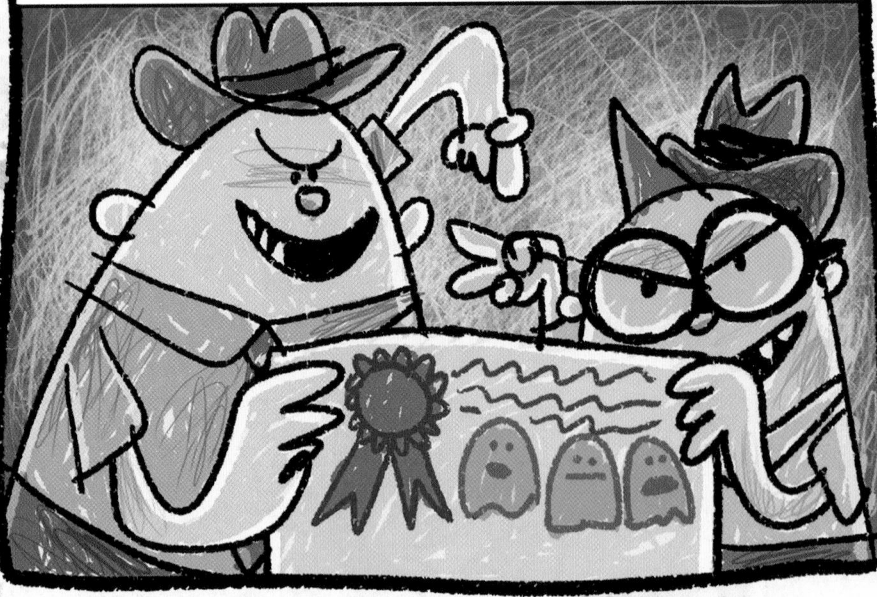

They came to town and warned everyone that Gumbalina Toothington, a giant ghost dentist, was on a rampage.

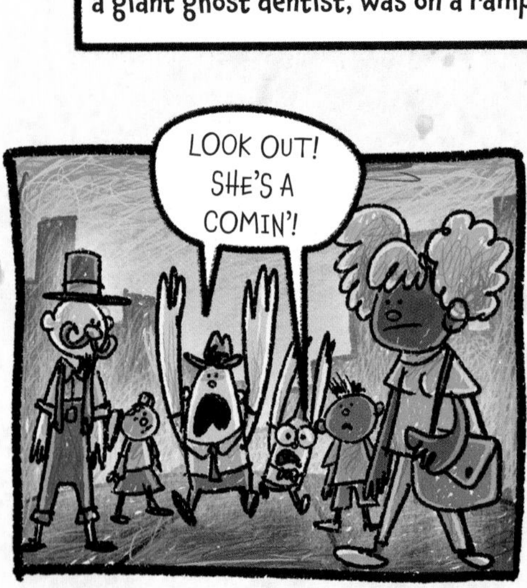
LOOK OUT! SHE'S A COMIN'!

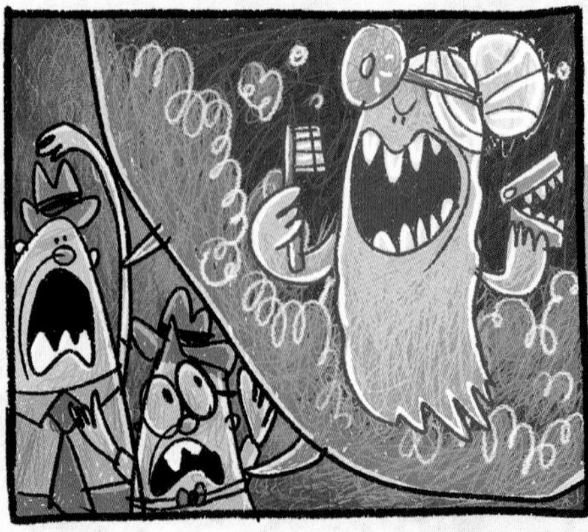

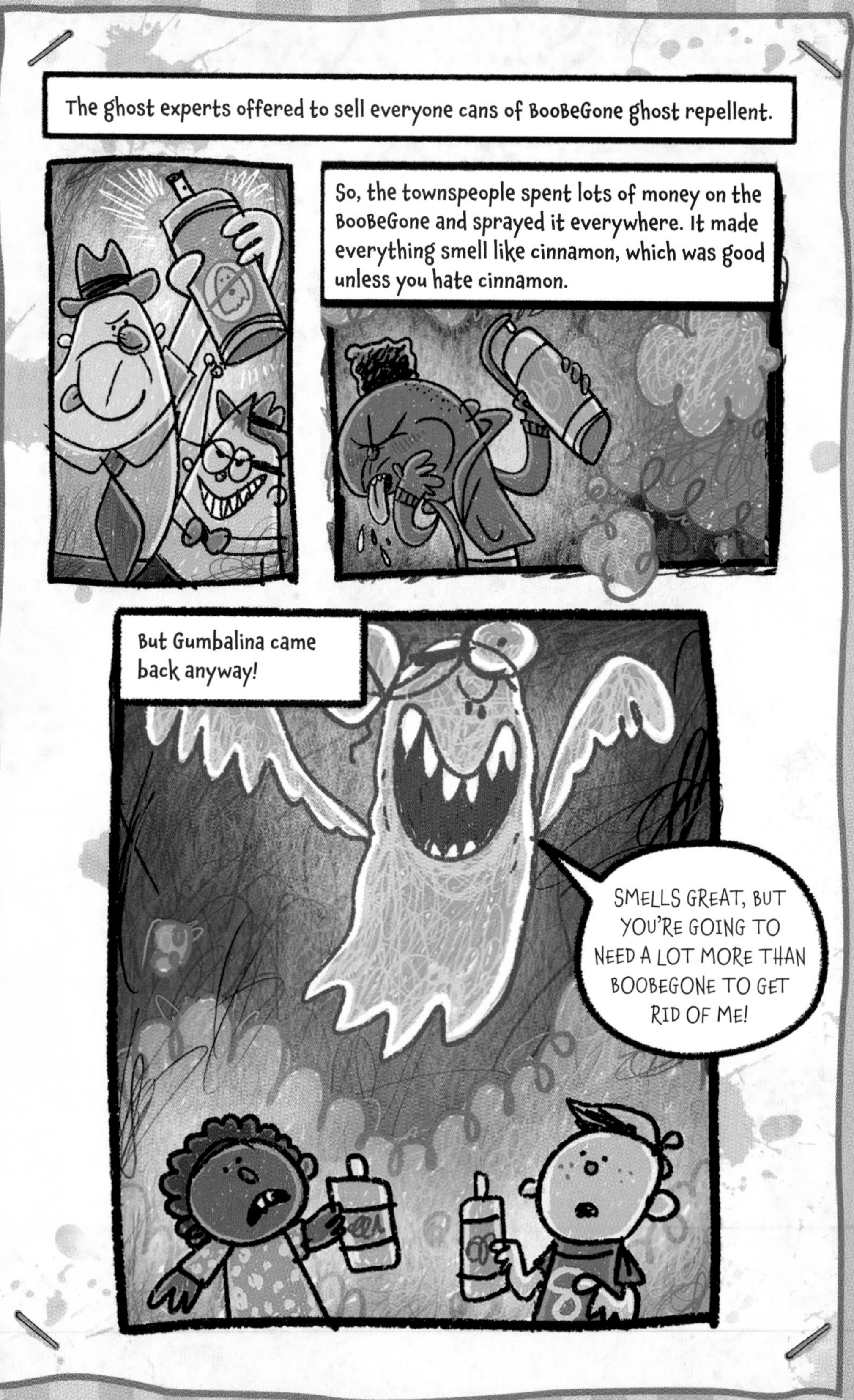
The ghost experts offered to sell everyone cans of BooBeGone ghost repellent.
So, the townspeople spent lots of money on the BooBeGone and sprayed it everywhere. It made everything smell like cinnamon, which was good unless you hate cinnamon.
But Gumbalina came back anyway!
SMELLS GREAT, BUT YOU'RE GOING TO NEED A LOT MORE THAN BOOBEGONE TO GET RID OF ME!

Luckily, Captain Underpants came because he thought he smelled cinnamon buns. But when he got to the town, did he find cinnamon buns? No! He found Gumbalina instead!

YOU KNOW THE DRILL, RIGHT? BECAUSE YOUR TEETH ARE ABOUT TO!

Captain Underpants wasn't about to give up that easily, though. He took out his undie-chucks (which are nunchucks made of undies) and twirled them all around the ghost.

WHIR-WHIR!

WHIR-WHIR!

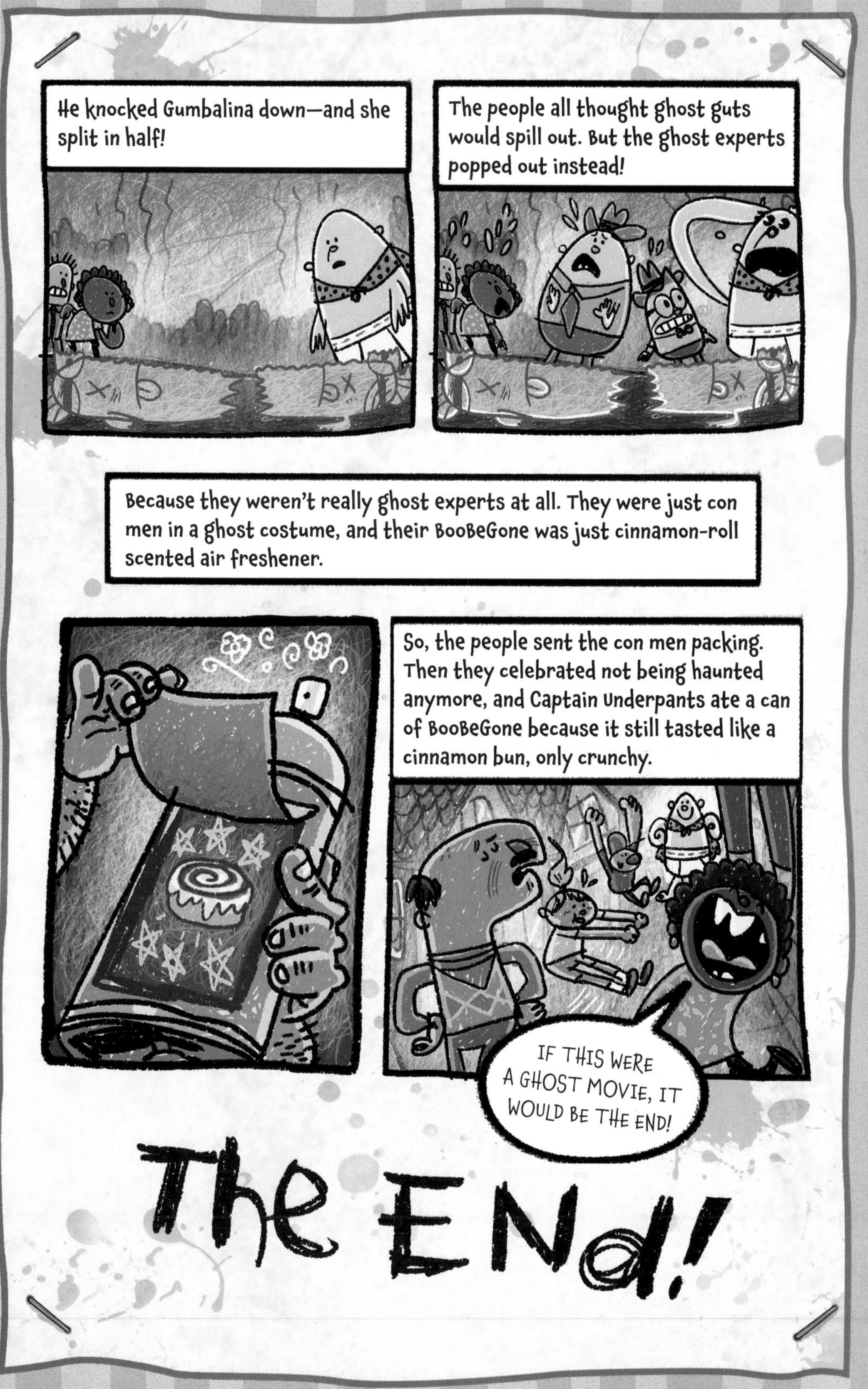
He knocked Gumbalina down—and she split in half!
The people all thought ghost guts would spill out. But the ghost experts popped out instead!
Because they weren't really ghost experts at all. They were just con men in a ghost costume, and their BooBeGone was just cinnamon-roll scented air freshener.
So, the people sent the con men packing. Then they celebrated not being haunted anymore, and Captain Underpants ate a can of BooBeGone because it still tasted like a cinnamon bun, only crunchy.
IF THIS WERE A GHOST MOVIE, IT WOULD BE THE END!
The End!

CHAPTER 4

NOTHING COMPARES TO CHEW

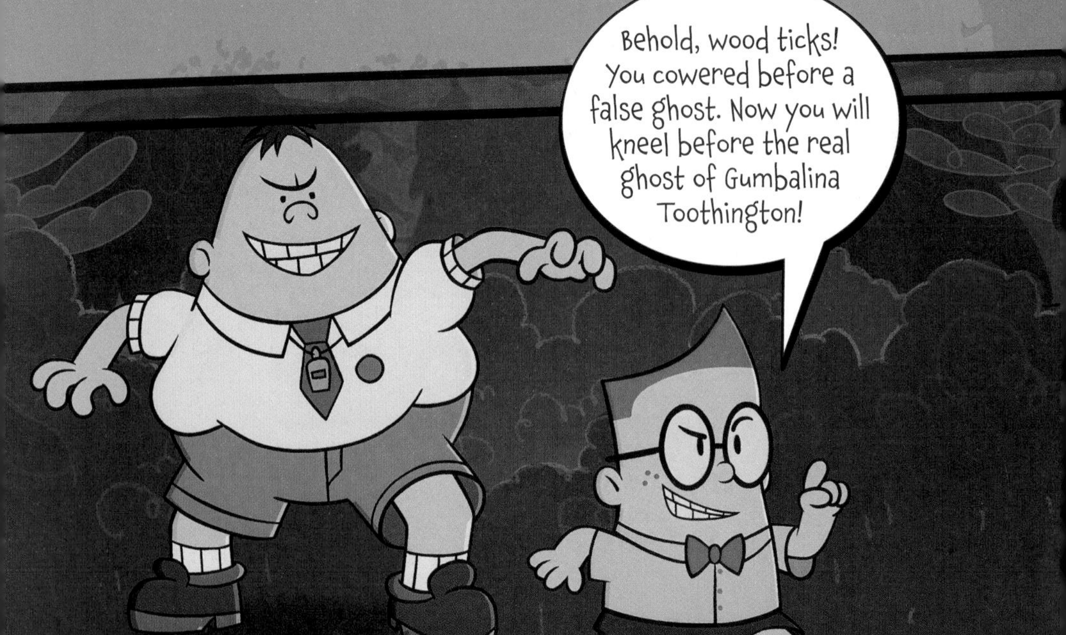
Behold, wood ticks! You cowered before a false ghost. Now you will kneel before the real ghost of Gumbalina Toothington!

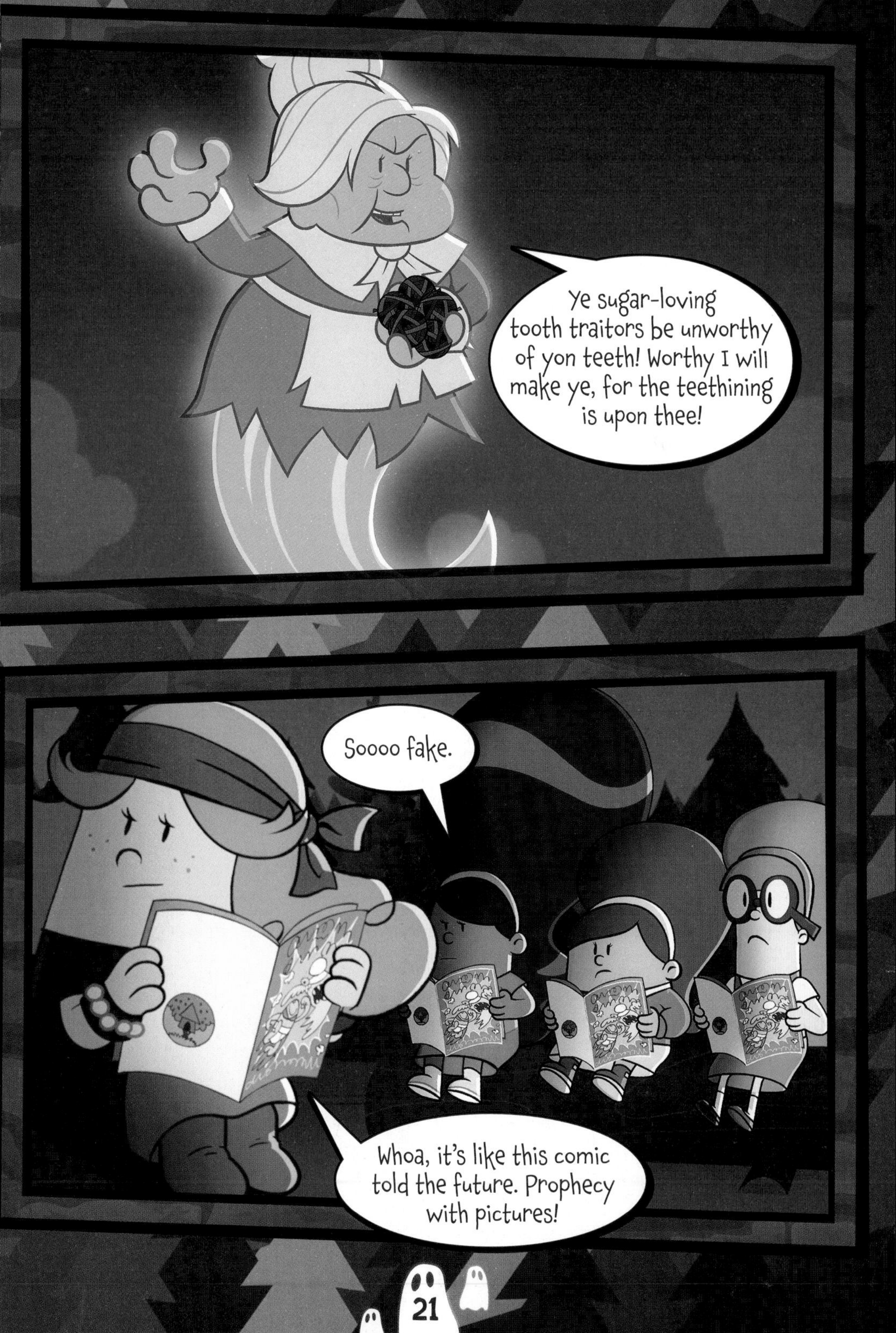
Ye sugar-loving tooth traitors be unworthy of yon teeth! Worthy I will make ye, for the teethining is upon thee!
Soooo fake.
Whoa, it's like this comic told the future. Prophecy with pictures!

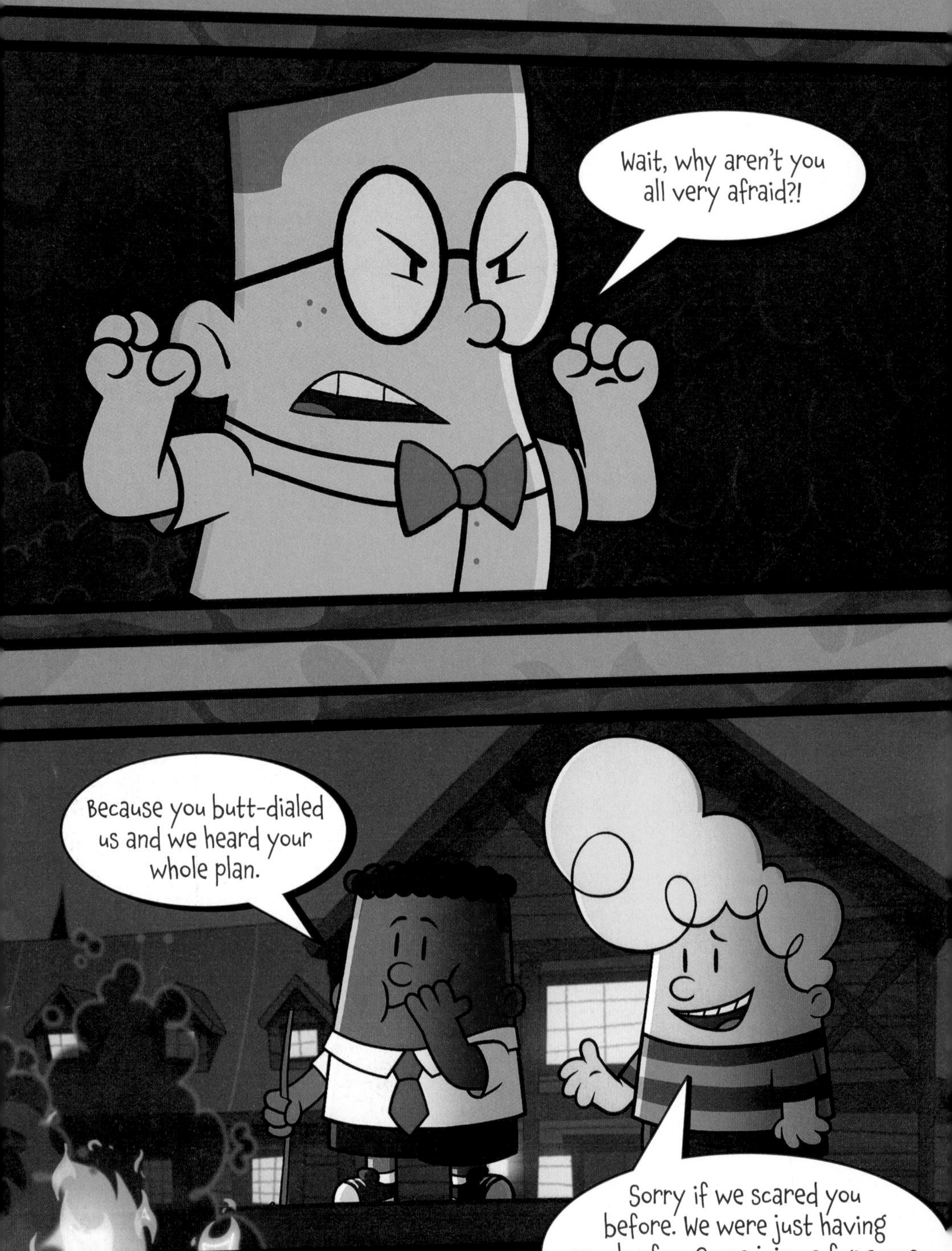
Wait, why aren't you all very afraid?!
Because you butt-dialed us and we heard your whole plan.
Sorry if we scared you before. We were just having spooky fun. Come join us for some campfire pizza. We saved you a slice!

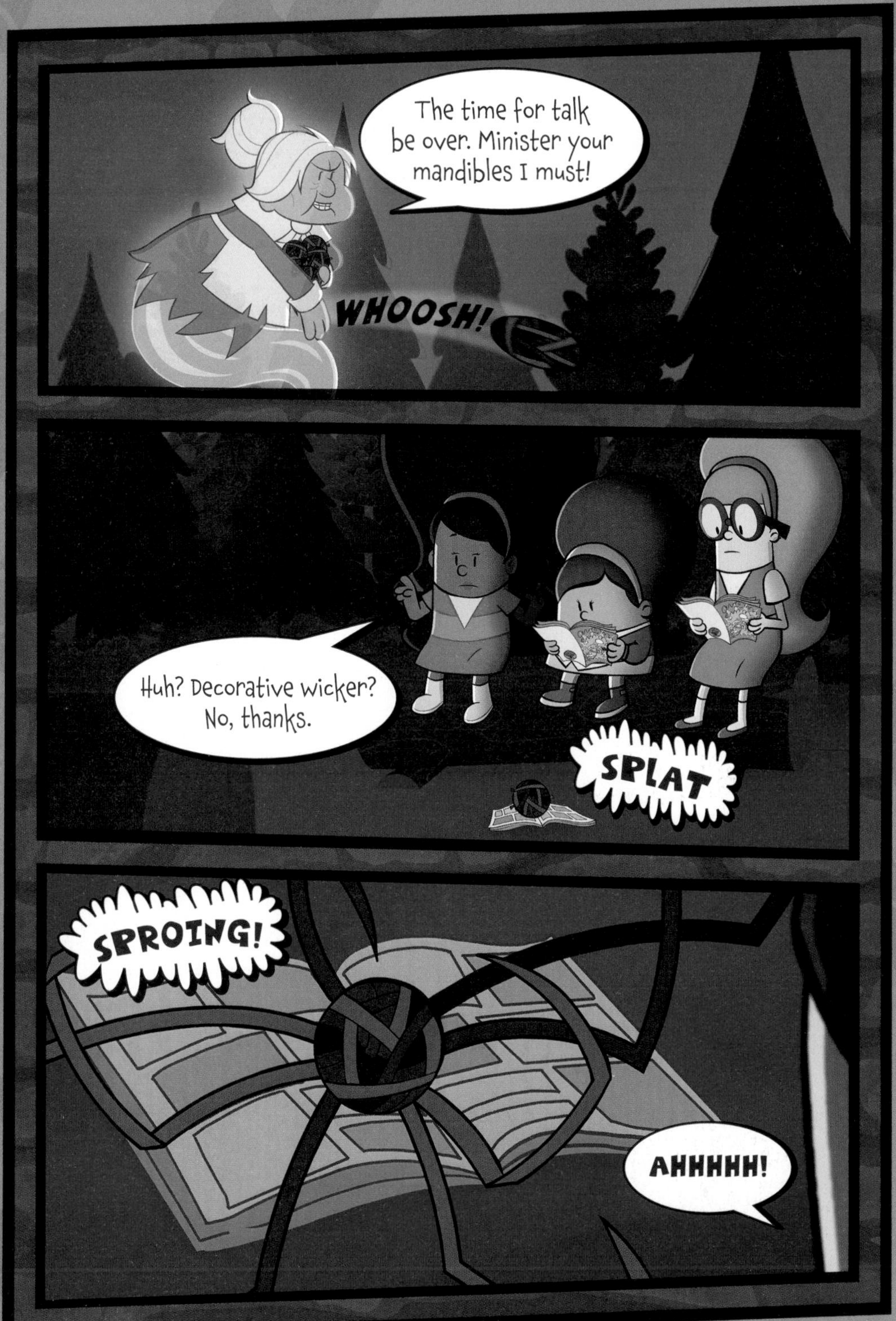
The time for talk be over. Minister your mandibles I must!
WHOOSH!
Huh? Decorative wicker? No, thanks.
SPLAT
SPROING!
AHHHHH!

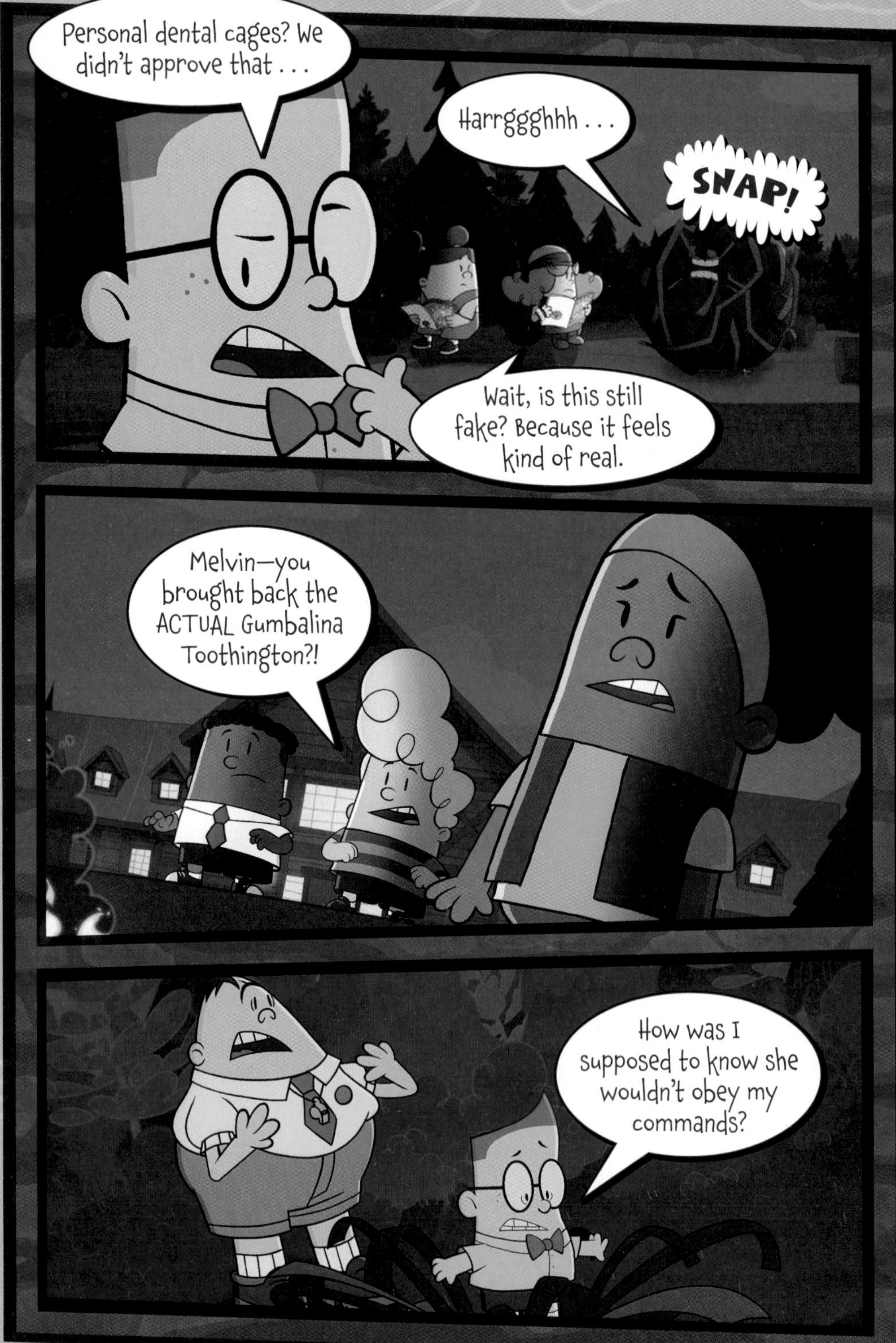
Personal dental cages? We didn't approve that . . .
Harrgggghhh . . .
SNAP!
Wait, is this still fake? Because it feels kind of real.
Melvin—you brought back the ACTUAL Gumbalina Toothington?!
How was I supposed to know she wouldn't obey my commands?

CHAPTER 5
SCARE-O-RAMA

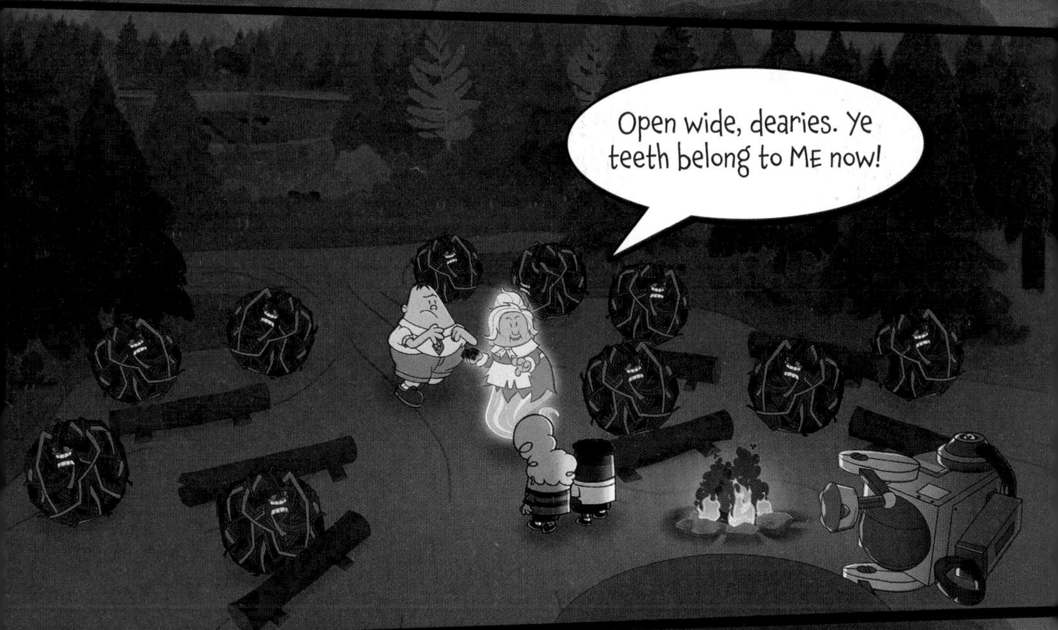
Open wide, dearies. Ye teeth belong to ME now!

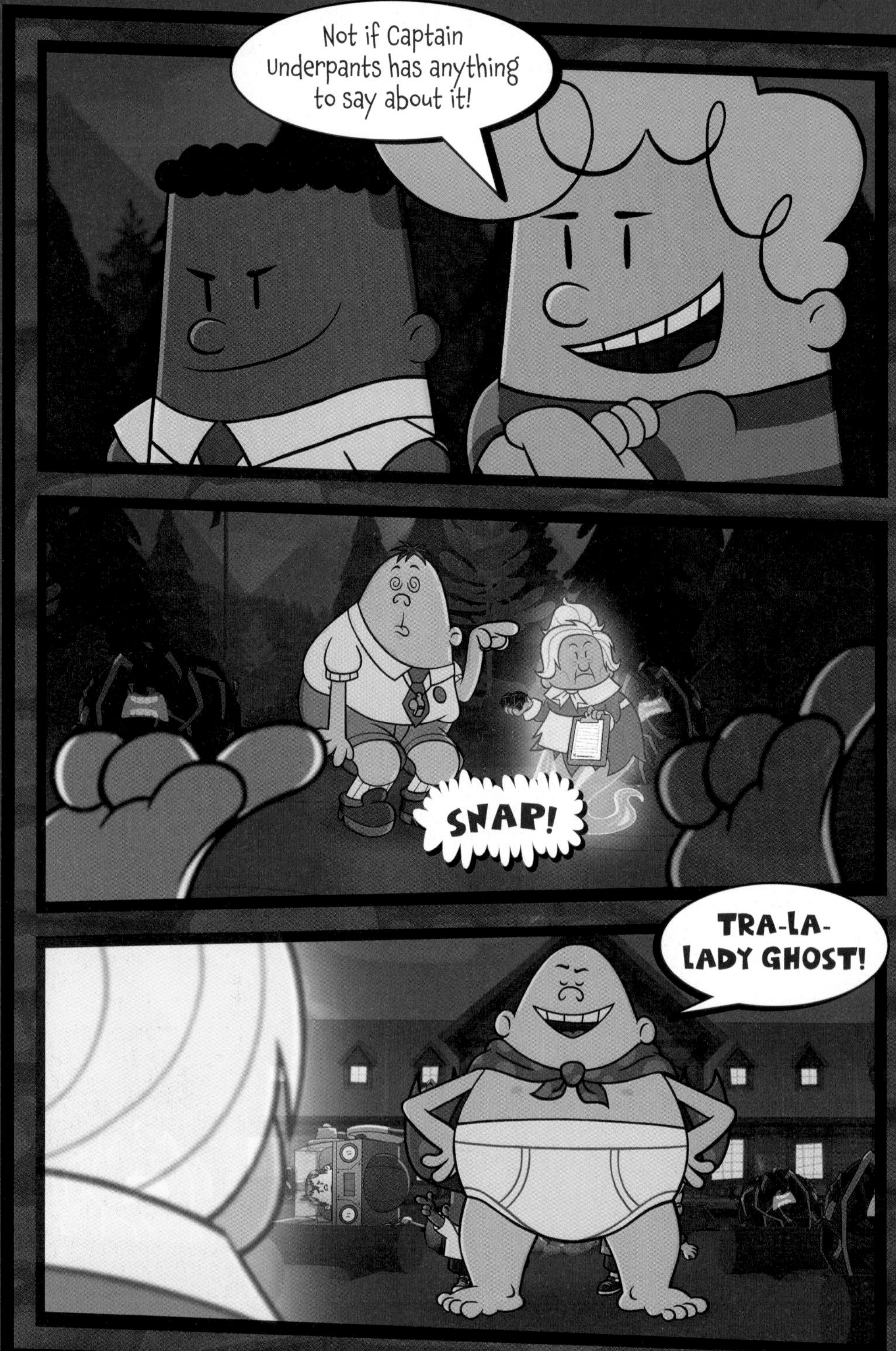
Not if Captain Underpants has anything to say about it!
SNAP!
TRA-LA-LADY GHOST!

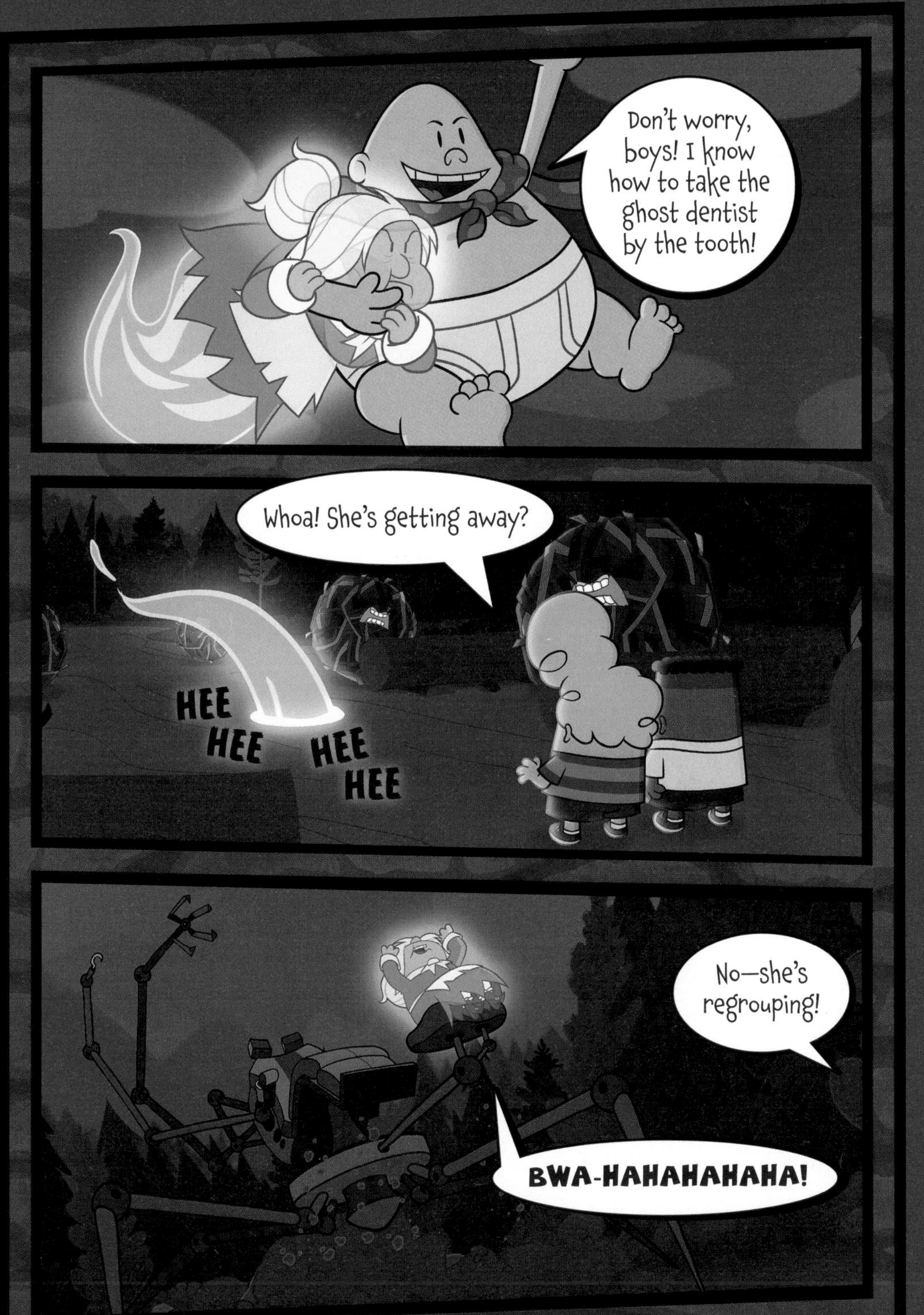
Don't worry, boys! I know how to take the ghost dentist by the tooth!
Whoa! She's getting away?
HEE HEE HEE HEE
No—she's regrouping!
BWA-HAHAHAHAHA!

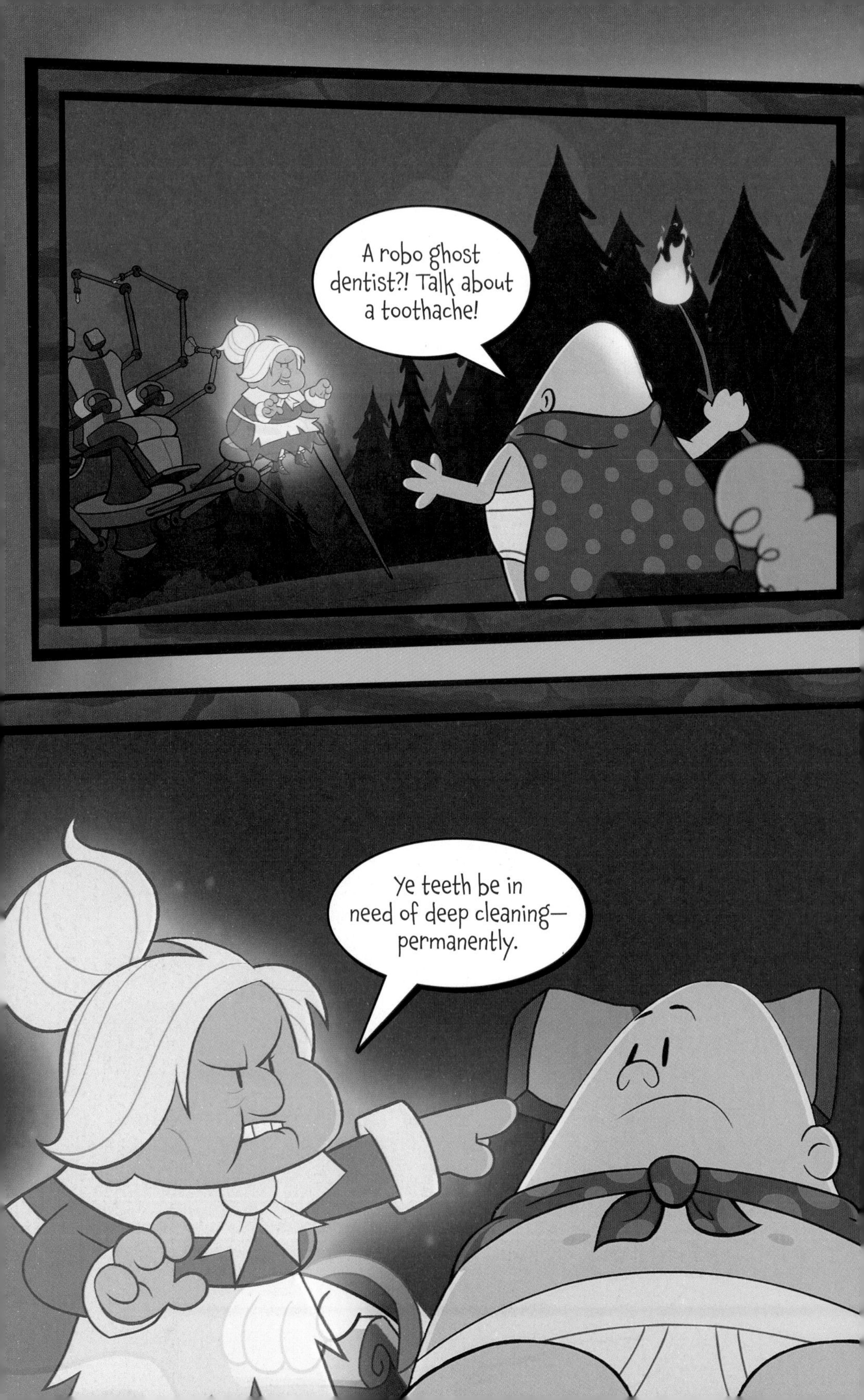
A robo ghost dentist?! Talk about a toothache!
Ye teeth be in need of deep cleaning—permanently.

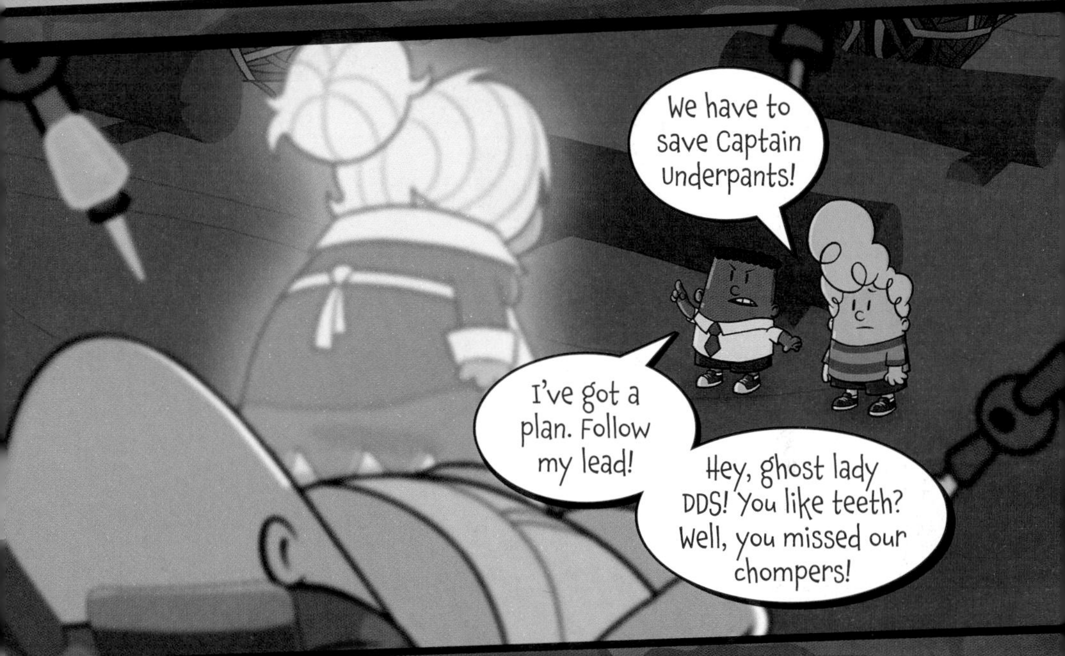
We have to save Captain Underpants!
I've got a plan. Follow my lead!
Hey, ghost lady DDS! You like teeth? Well, you missed our chompers!

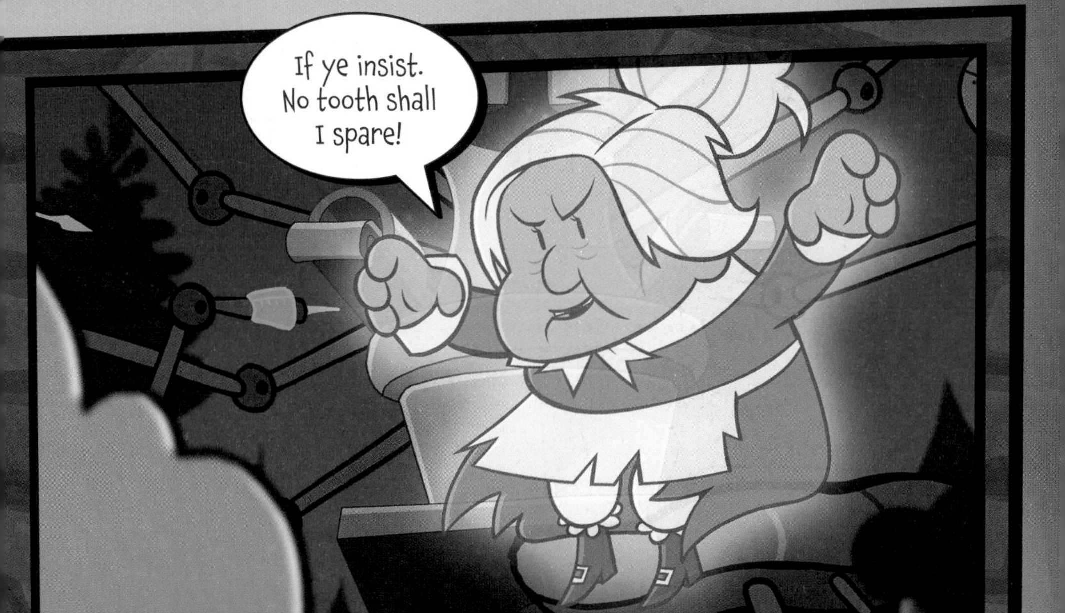
If ye insist. No tooth shall I spare!

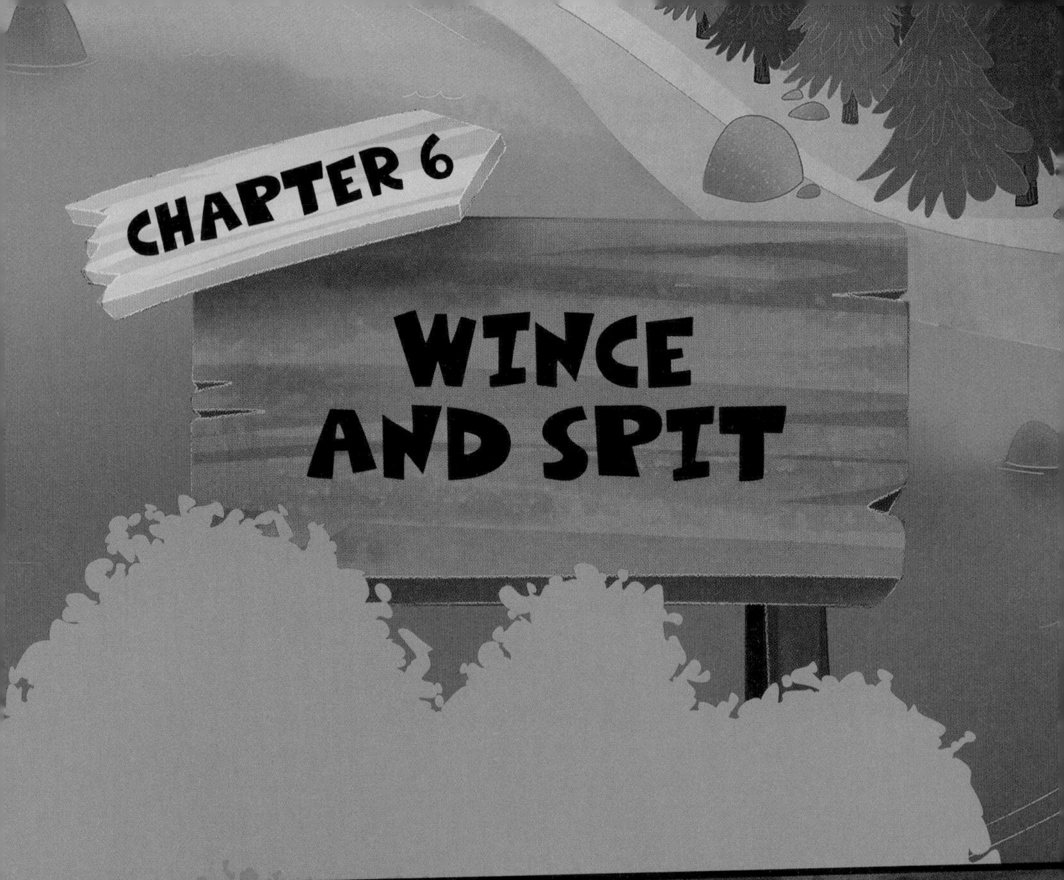
CHAPTER 6
WINCE AND SPIT

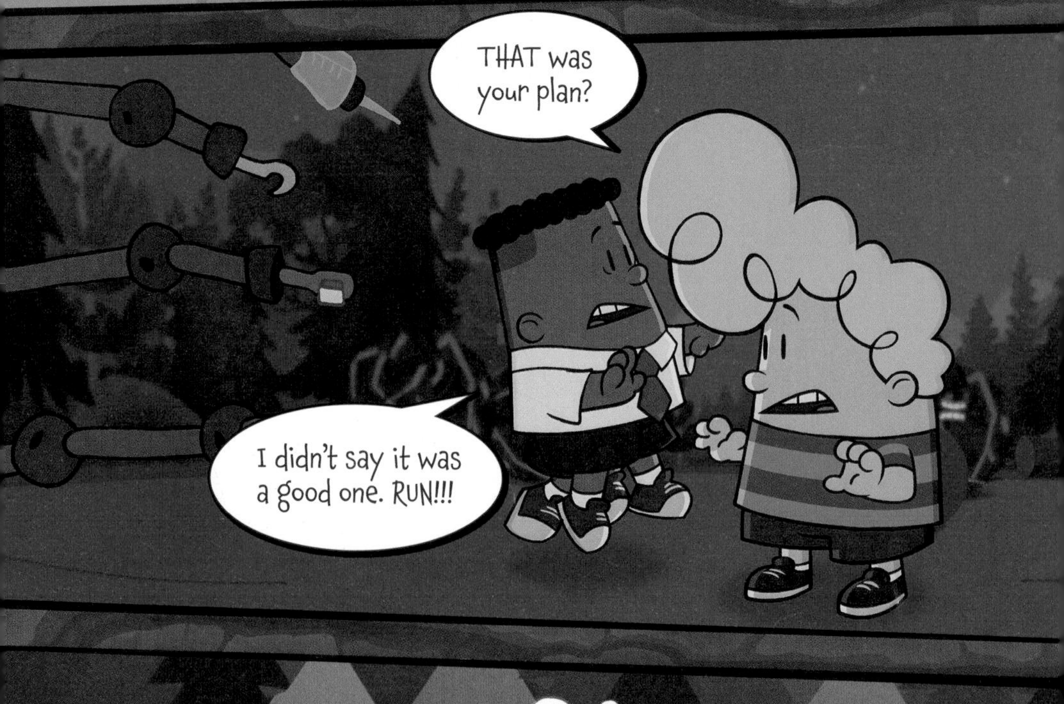
THAT was your plan?
I didn't say it was a good one. RUN!!!

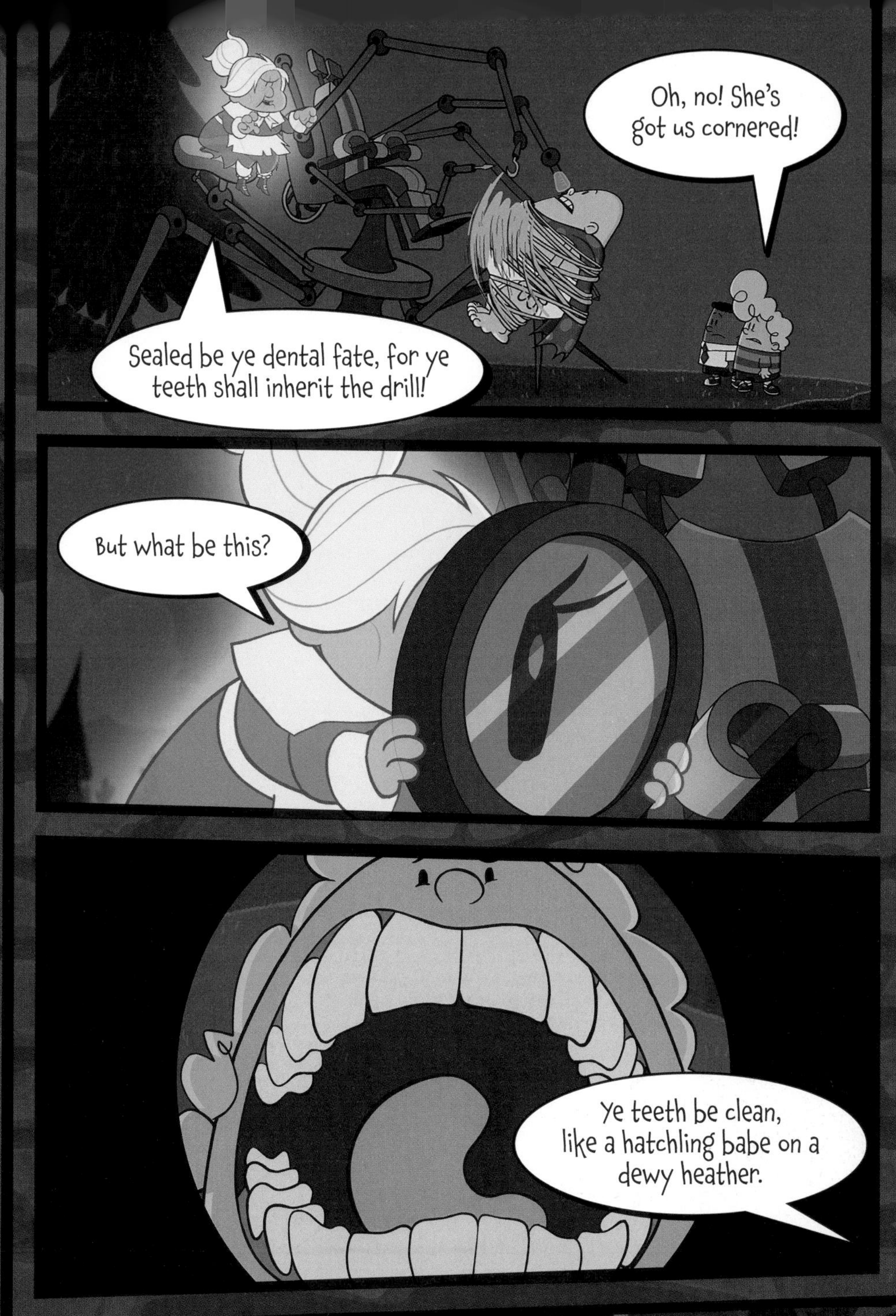
Oh, no! She's got us cornered!
Sealed be ye dental fate, for ye teeth shall inherit the drill!
But what be this?
Ye teeth be clean, like a hatchling babe on a dewy heather.

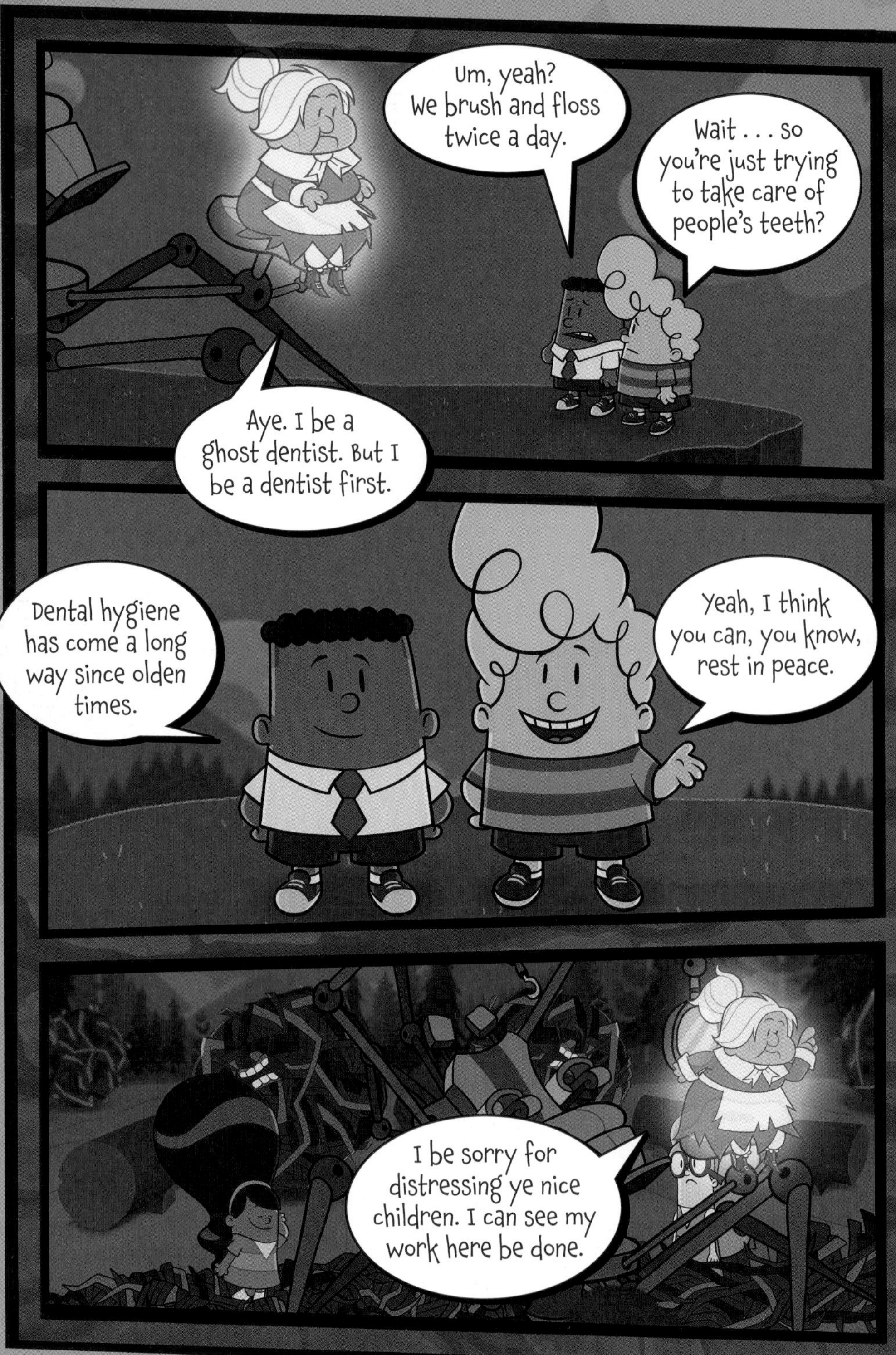
Um, yeah? We brush and floss twice a day.
Wait . . . so you're just trying to take care of people's teeth?
Aye. I be a ghost dentist. But I be a dentist first.
Dental hygiene has come a long way since olden times.
Yeah, I think you can, you know, rest in peace.
I be sorry for distressing ye nice children. I can see my work here be done.

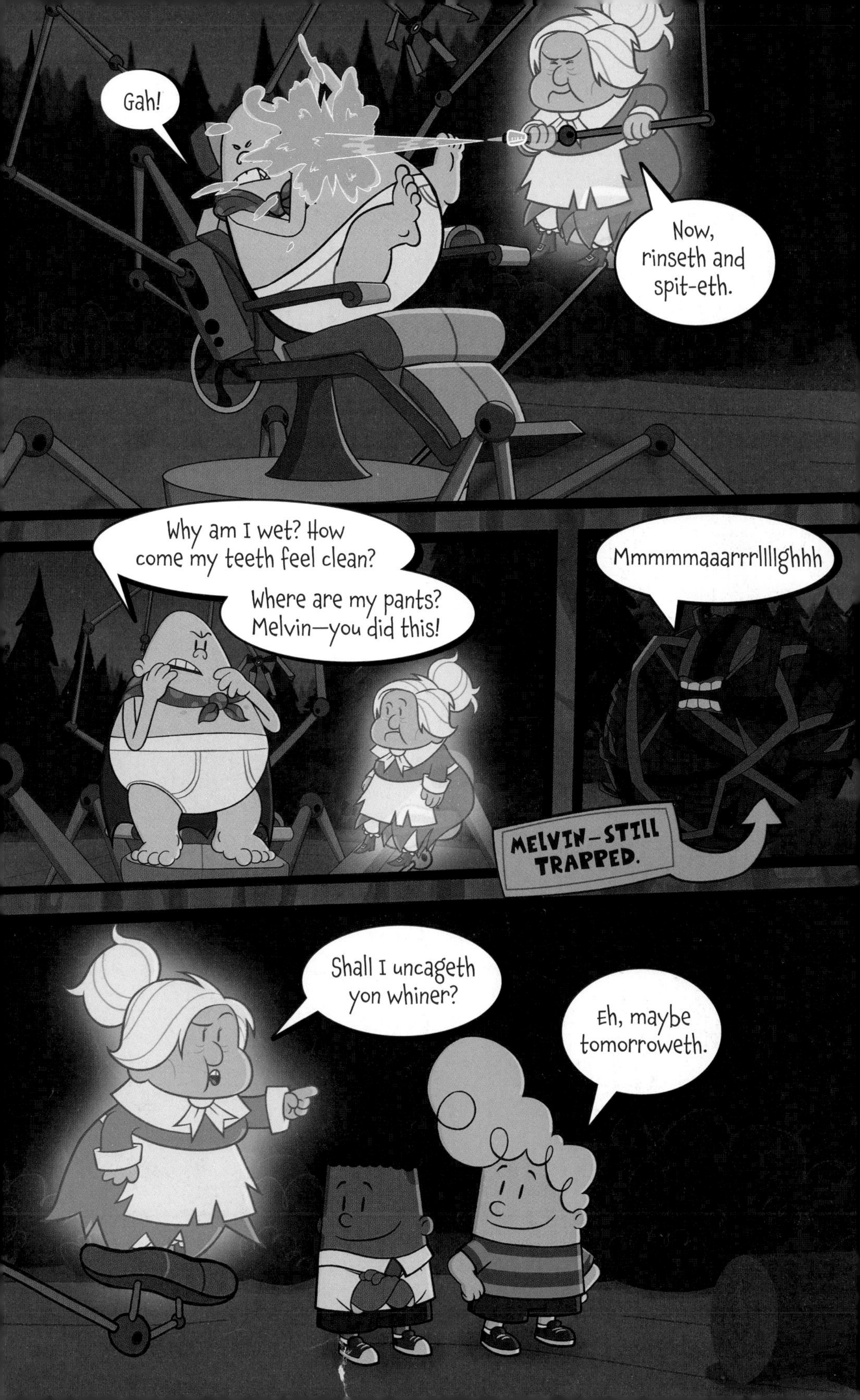
Gah!
Now, rinseth and spit-eth.
Why am I wet? How come my teeth feel clean?
Where are my pants? Melvin—you did this!
Mmmmmaaarrrlllghhh
MELVIN—STILL TRAPPED.
Shall I uncageth yon whiner?
Eh, maybe tomorroweth.

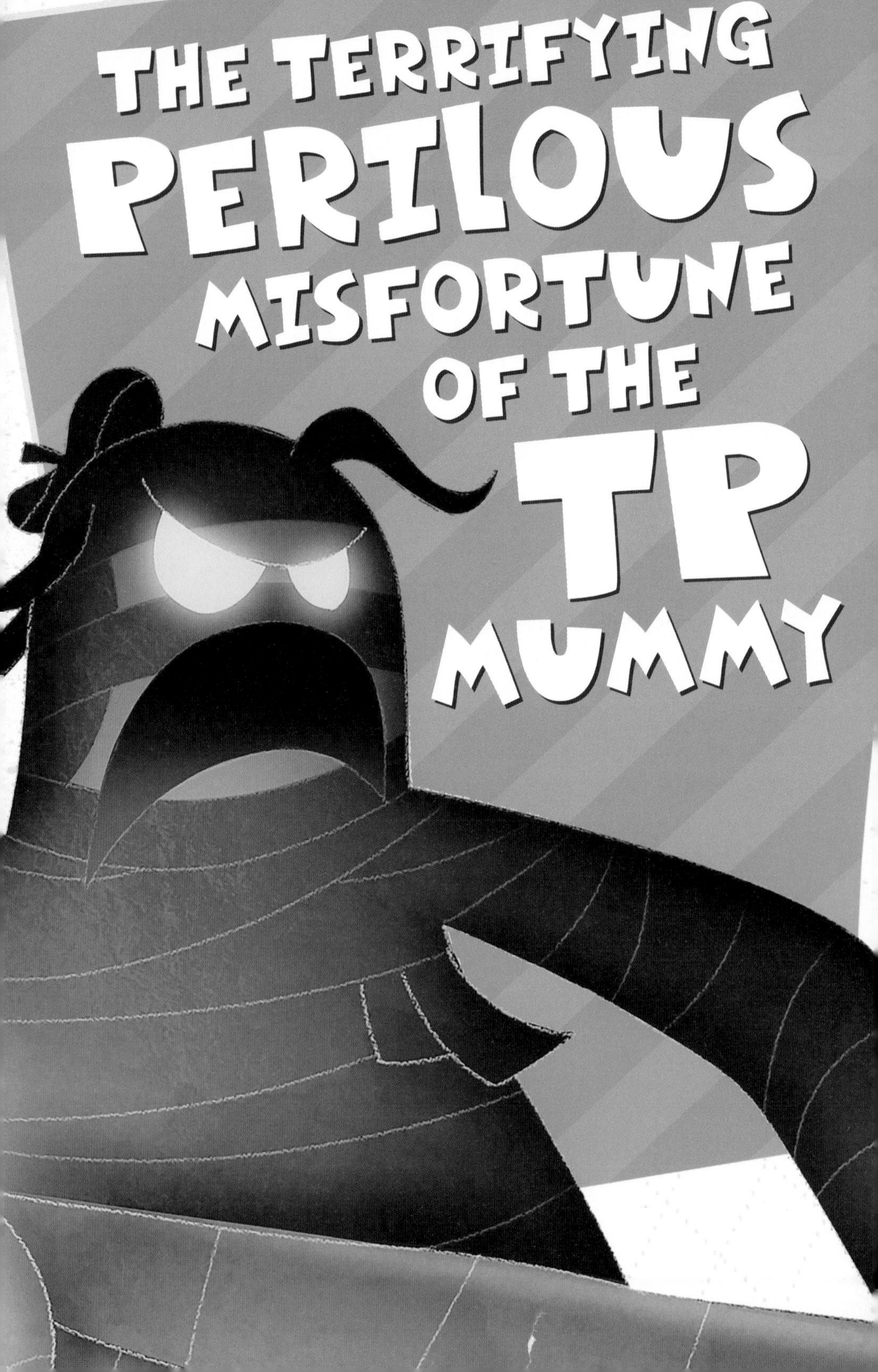
THE TERRIFYING
PERILOUS
MISFORTUNE
OF THE
TP
MUMMY

CHAPTER 1

TP TIME-OUT

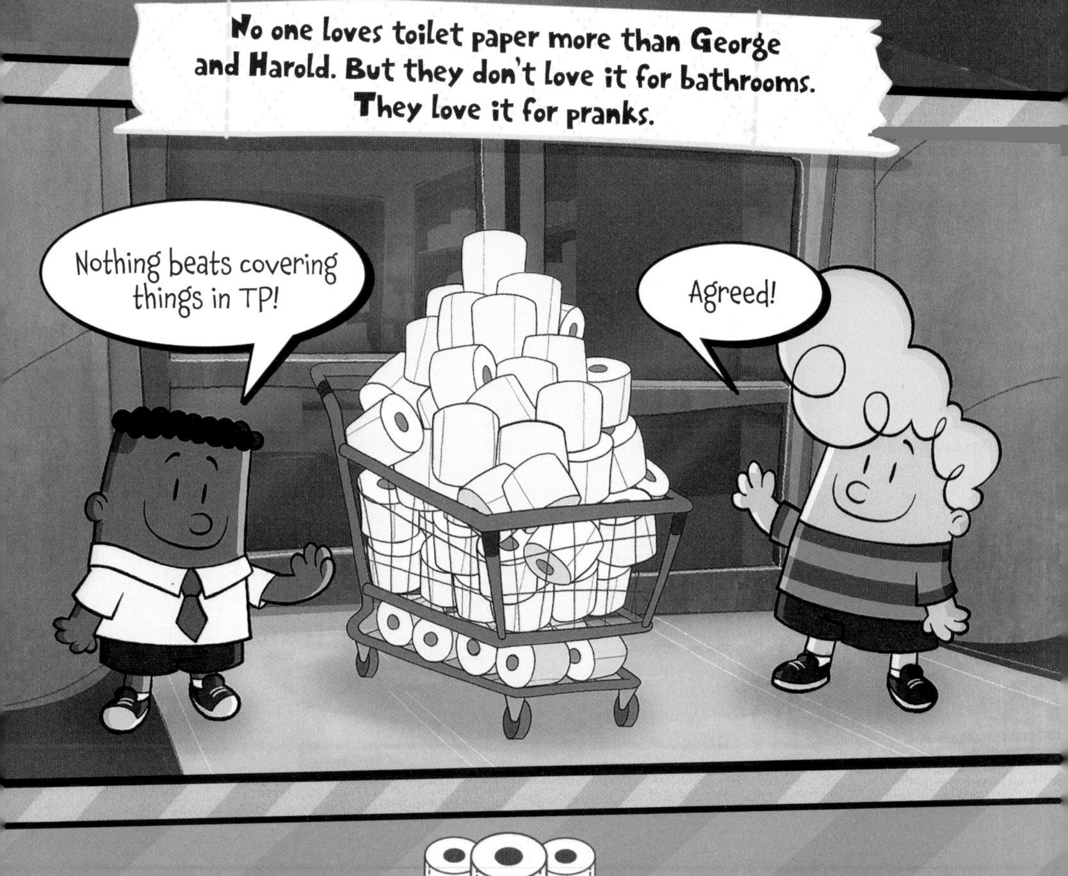

No one loves toilet paper more than George and Harold. But they don't love it for bathrooms. They love it for pranks.
Nothing beats covering things in TP!
Agreed!

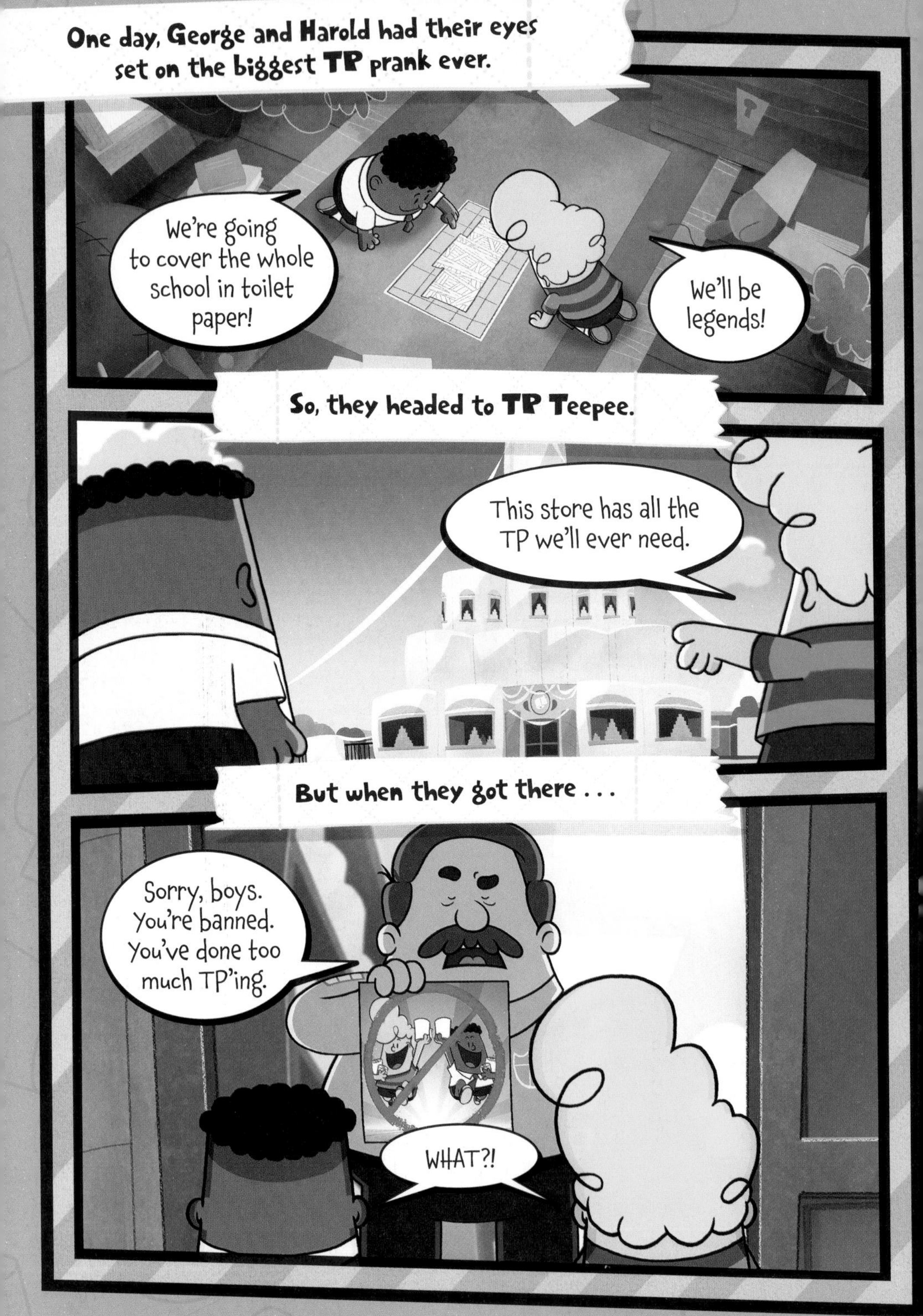
One day, George and Harold had their eyes set on the biggest TP prank ever.
We're going to cover the whole school in toilet paper!
We'll be legends!
So, they headed to TP Teepee.
This store has all the TP we'll ever need.
But when they got there . . .
Sorry, boys. You're banned. You've done too much TP'ing.
WHAT?!

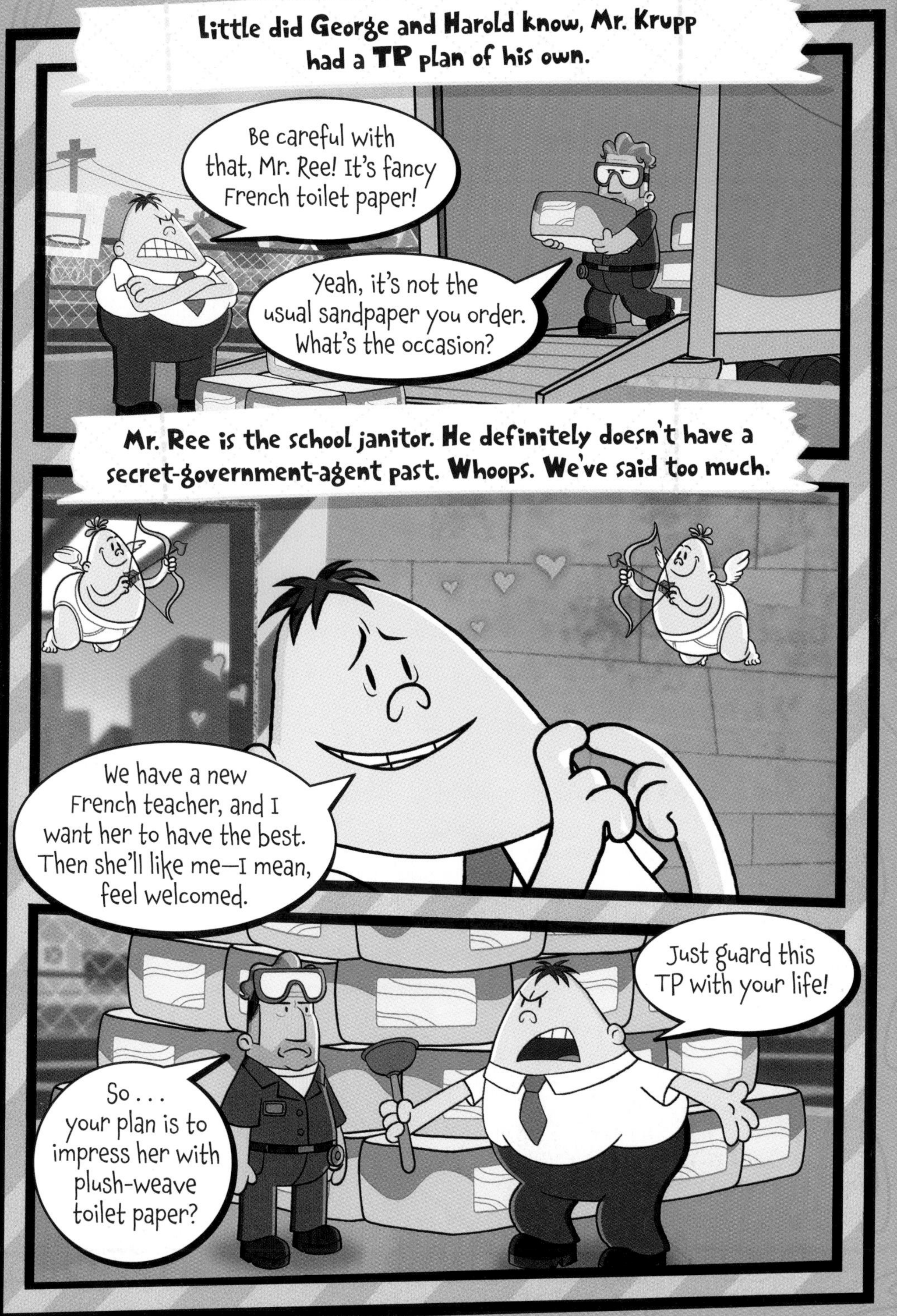
Little did George and Harold know, Mr. Krupp had a TP plan of his own.
Be careful with that, Mr. Ree! It's fancy French toilet paper!
Yeah, it's not the usual sandpaper you order. What's the occasion?
Mr. Ree is the school janitor. He definitely doesn't have a secret-government-agent past. Whoops. We've said too much.
We have a new French teacher, and I want her to have the best. Then she'll like me—I mean, feel welcomed.
Just guard this TP with your life!
So . . . your plan is to impress her with plush-weave toilet paper?

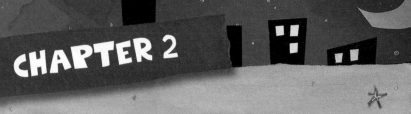

CHAPTER 2

KRUPPY LOVE

This is Ms. Yewh, the new French teacher.
She loves everything French.

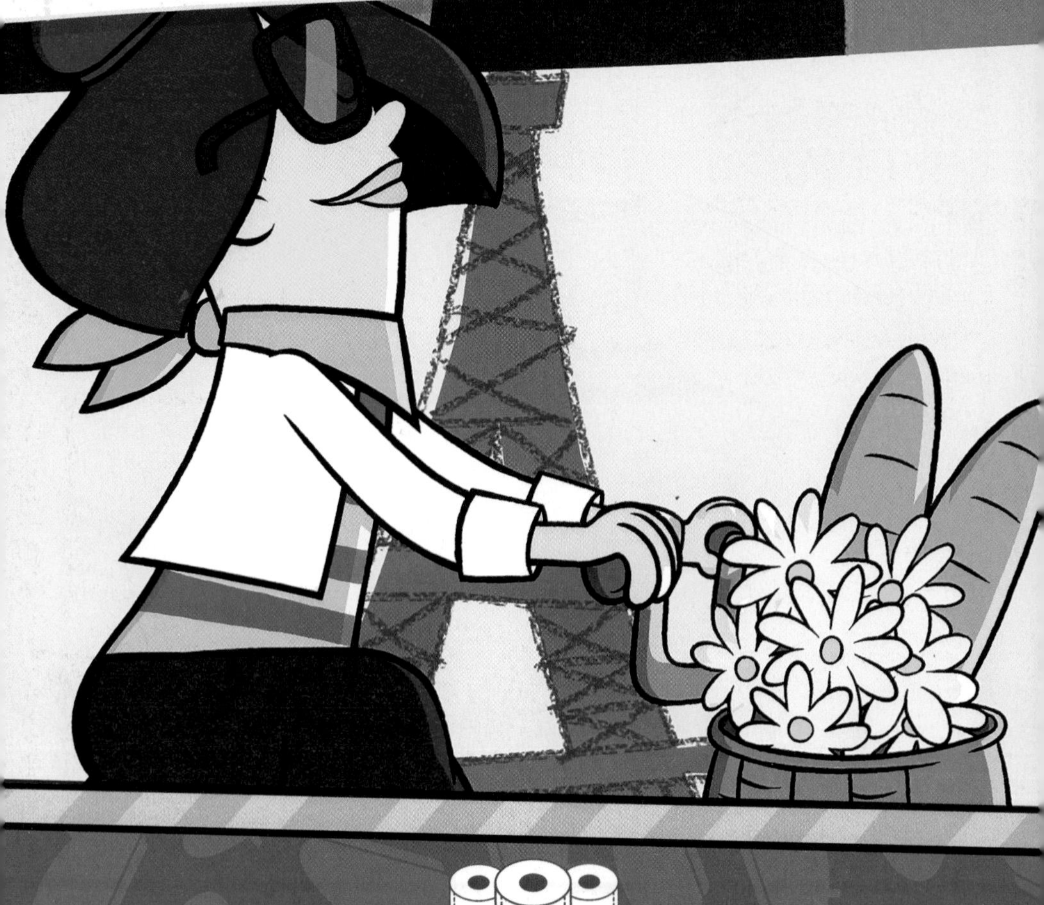

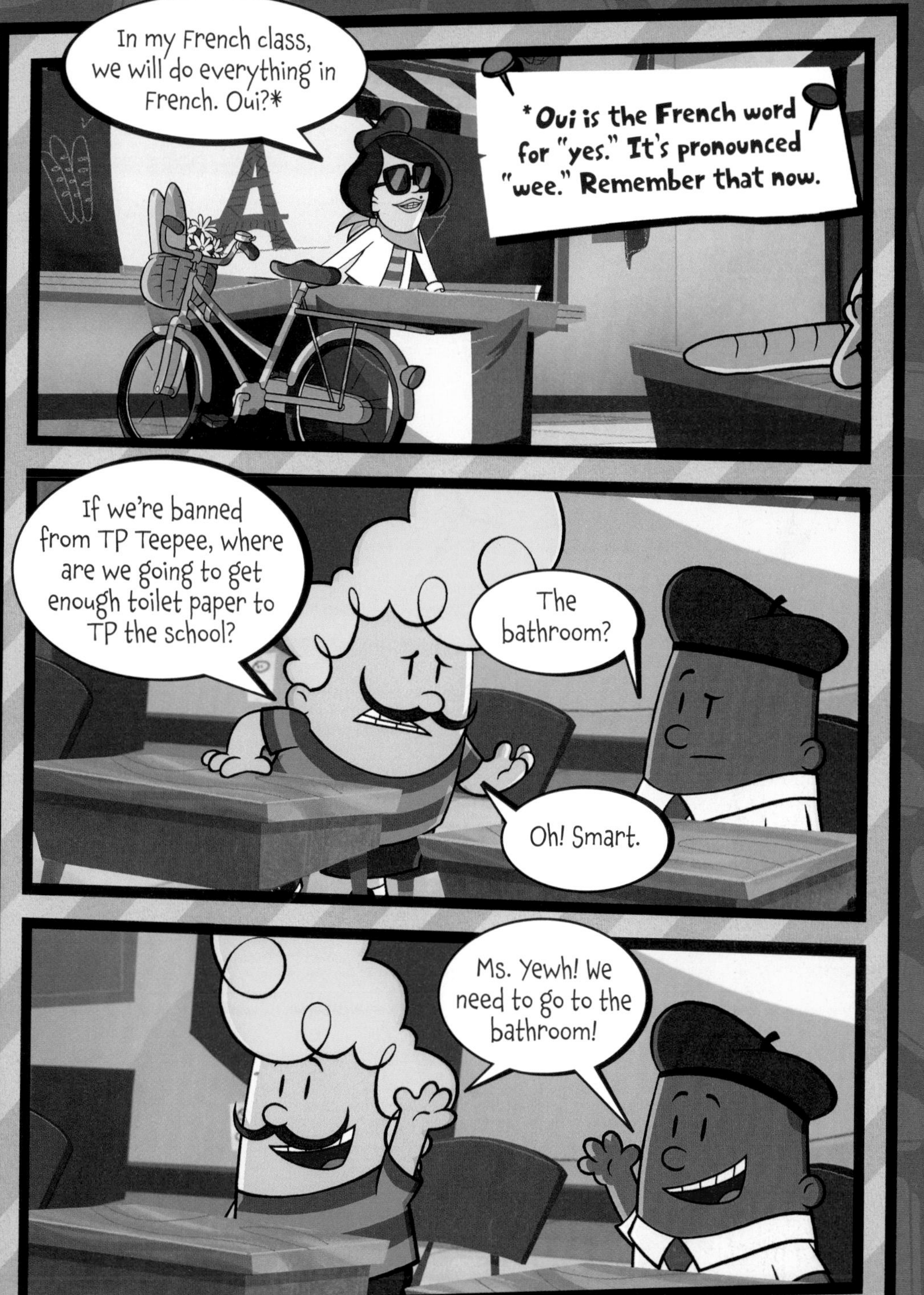
In my French class, we will do everything in French. Oui?*
*Oui is the French word for "yes." It's pronounced "wee." Remember that now.
If we're banned from TP Teepee, where are we going to get enough toilet paper to TP the school?
The bathroom?
Oh! Smart.
Ms. Yewh! We need to go to the bathroom!

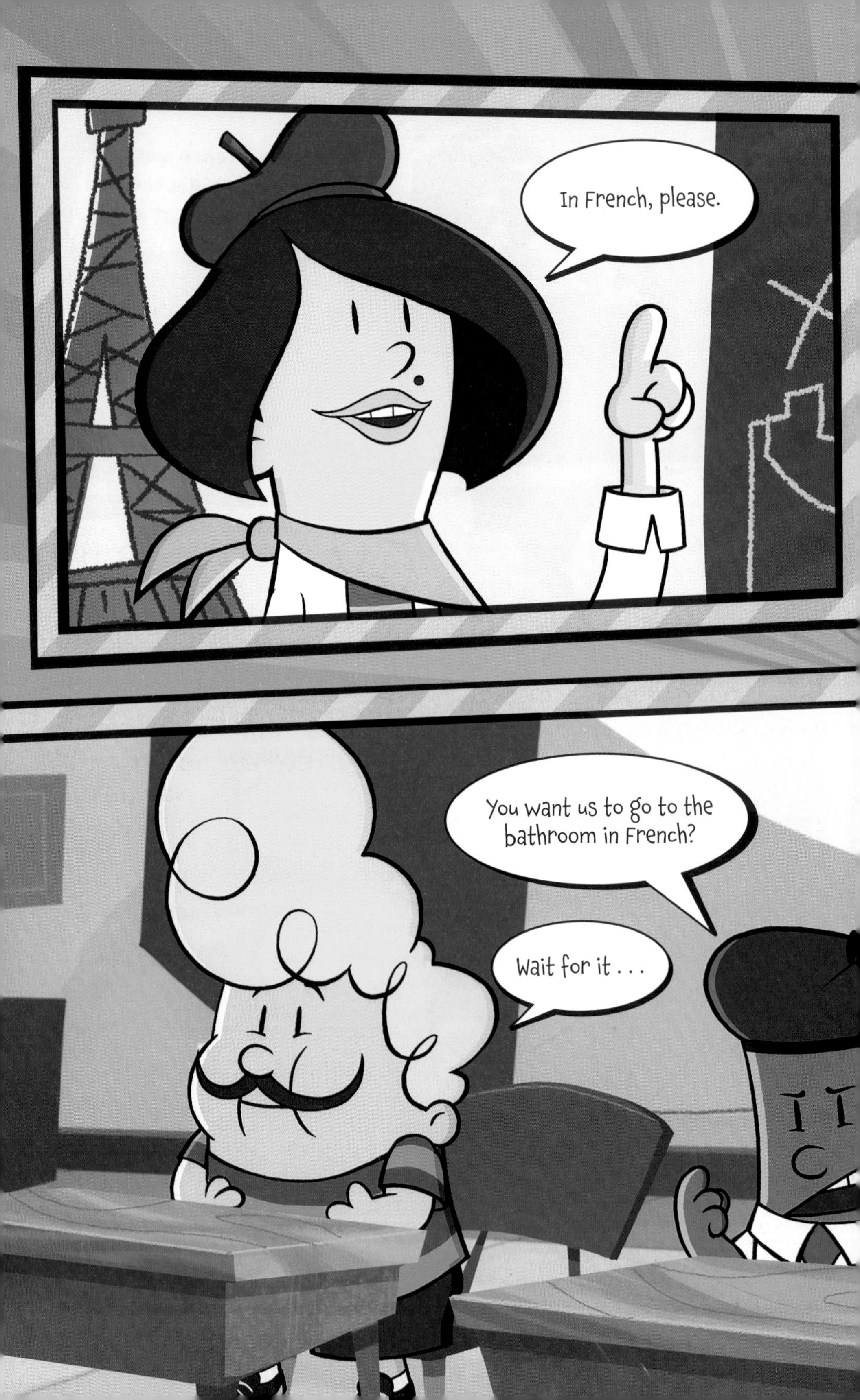
In French, please.
You want us to go to the bathroom in French?
Wait for it . . .

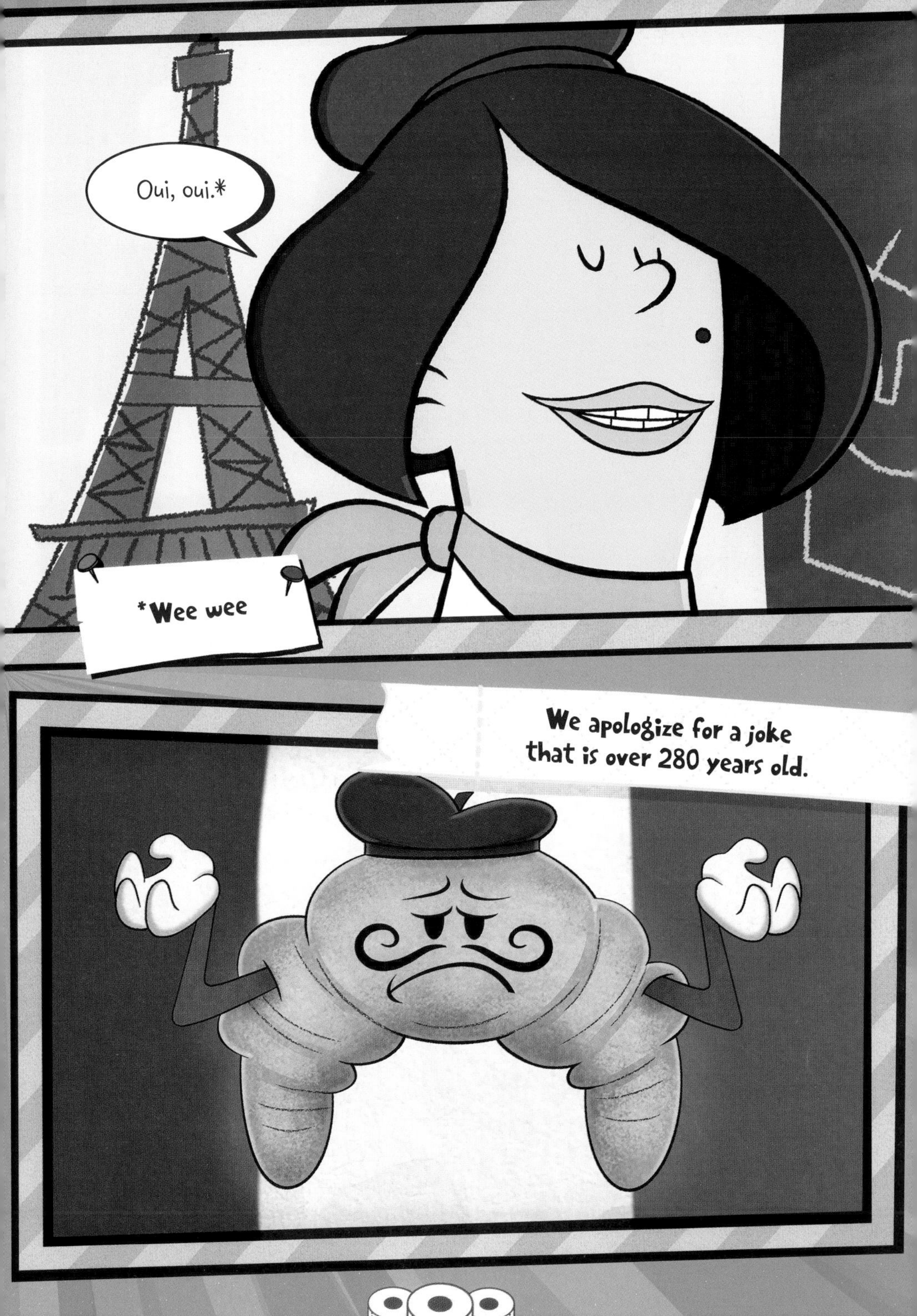
Oui, oui.*
*Wee wee
We apologize for a joke that is over 280 years old.

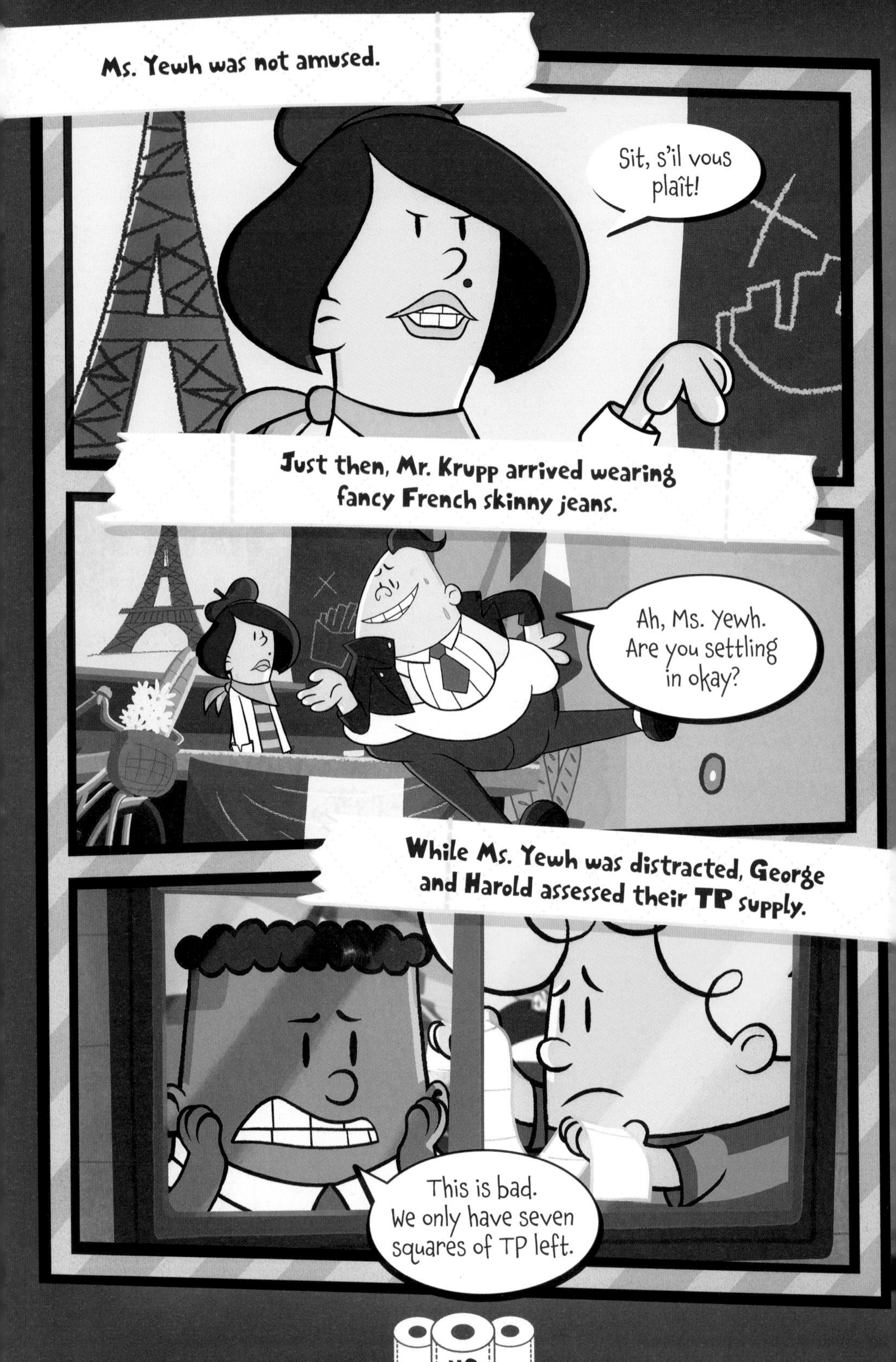
Ms. Yewh was not amused.
Sit, s'il vous plaît!
Just then, Mr. Krupp arrived wearing fancy French skinny jeans.
Ah, Ms. Yewh. Are you settling in okay?
While Ms. Yewh was distracted, George and Harold assessed their TP supply.
This is bad. We only have seven squares of TP left.

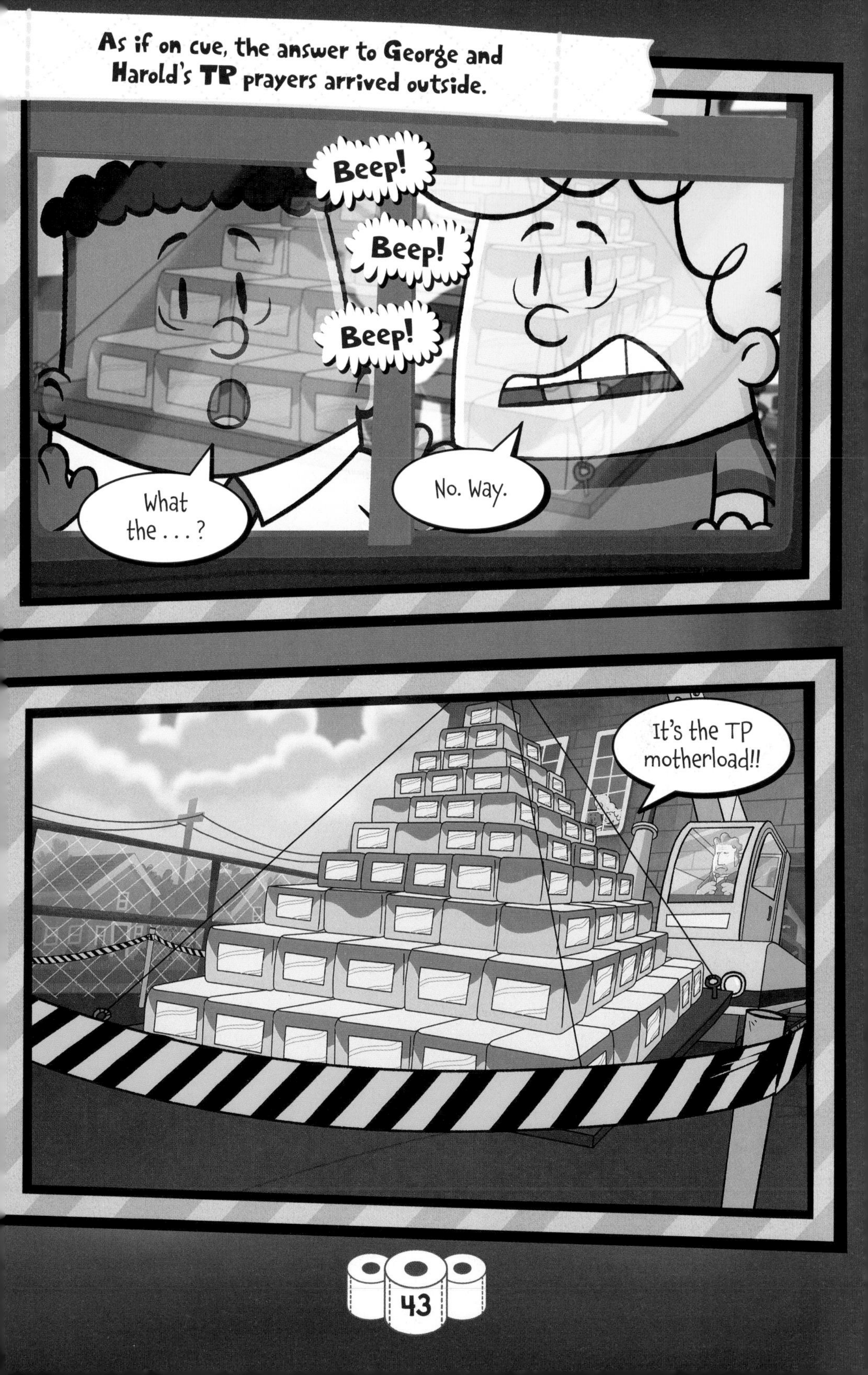
As if on cue, the answer to George and Harold's TP prayers arrived outside.
Beep!
Beep!
Beep!
What the . . . ?
No. Way.
It's the TP motherload!!

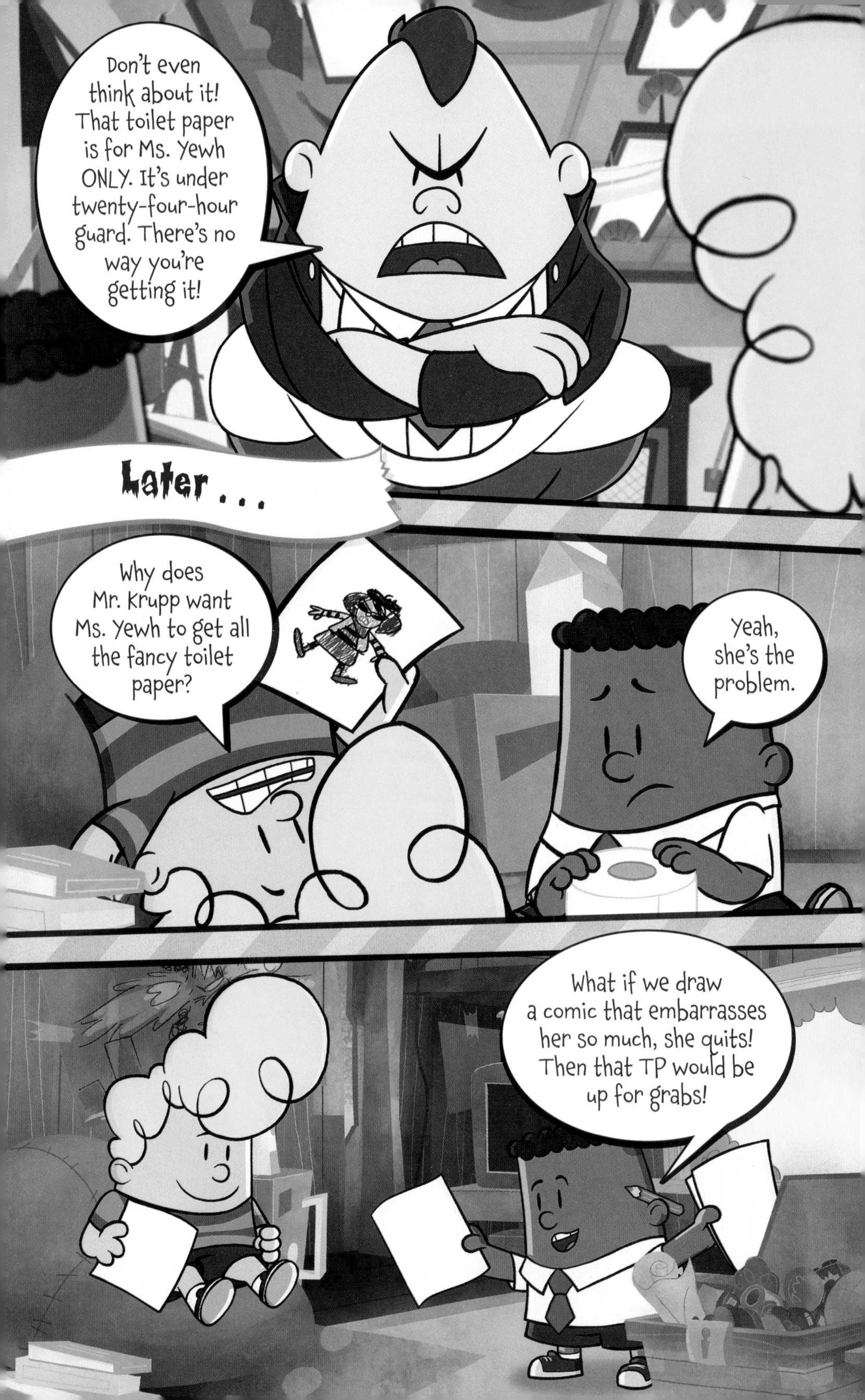

Don't even think about it! That toilet paper is for Ms. Yewh ONLY. It's under twenty-four-hour guard. There's no way you're getting it!
Later . . .
Why does Mr. Krupp want Ms. Yewh to get all the fancy toilet paper?
Yeah, she's the problem.
What if we draw a comic that embarrasses her so much, she quits! Then that TP would be up for grabs!

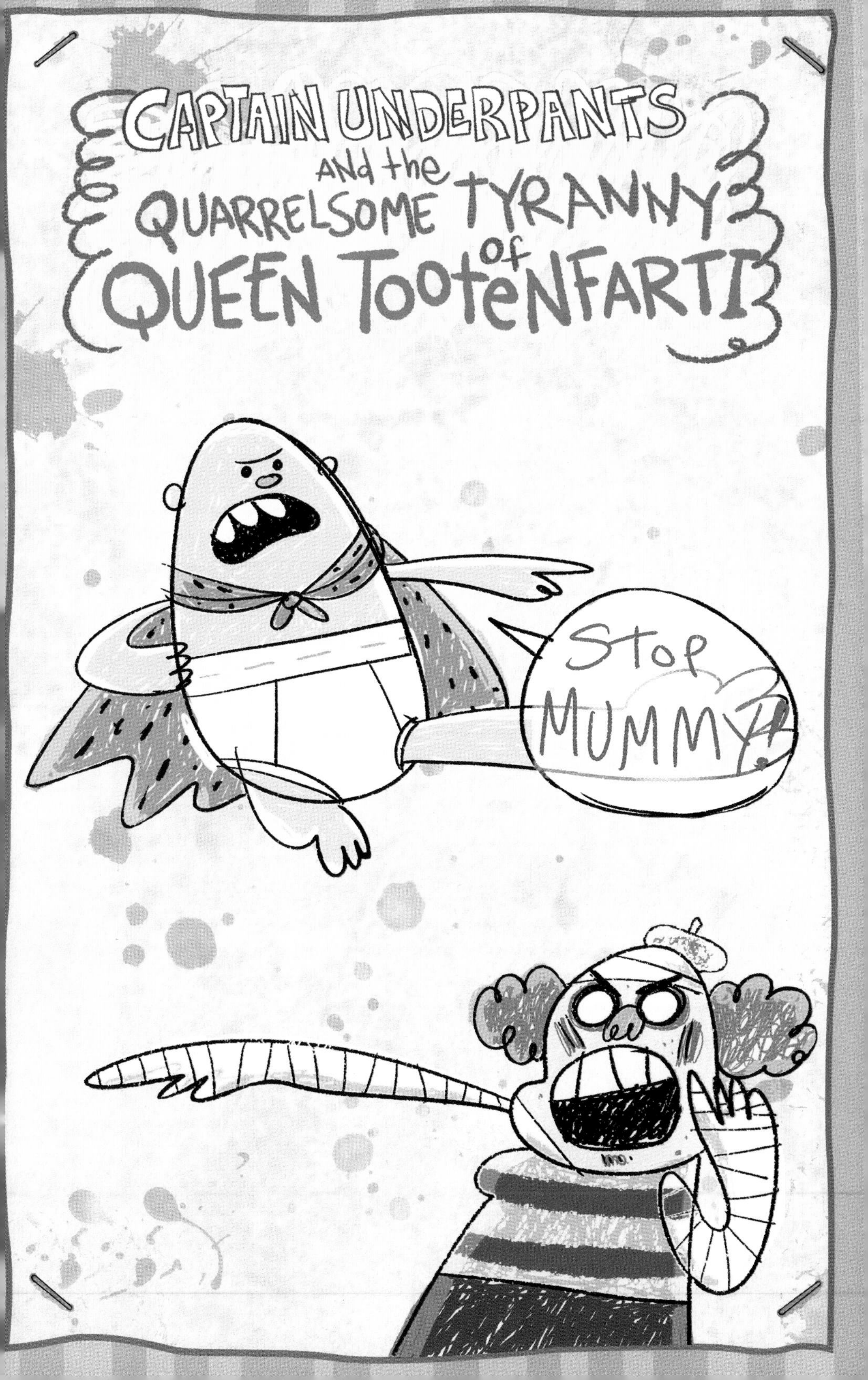
CAPTAIN UNDERPANTS
AND the
QUARRELSOME TYRANNY
of
QUEEN TOOTENFARTI
STOP MUMMY!

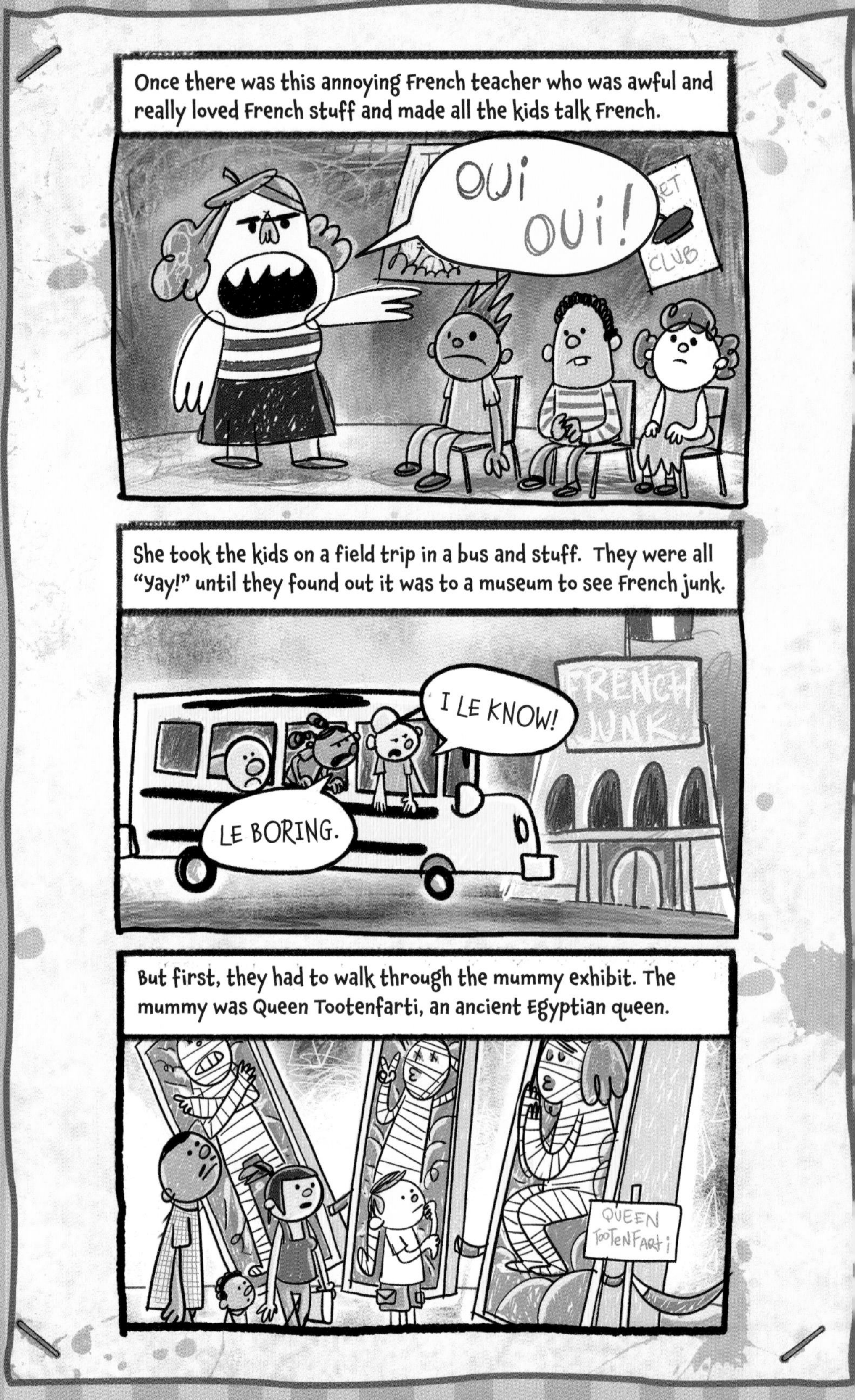
Once there was this annoying French teacher who was awful and really loved French stuff and made all the kids talk French.
OUI OUI!
CLUB
She took the kids on a field trip in a bus and stuff. They were all "Yay!" until they found out it was to a museum to see French junk.
I LE KNOW!
LE BORING.
FRENCH JUNK
But first, they had to walk through the mummy exhibit. The mummy was Queen Tootenfarti, an ancient Egyptian queen.
QUEEN TOOTENFARTi

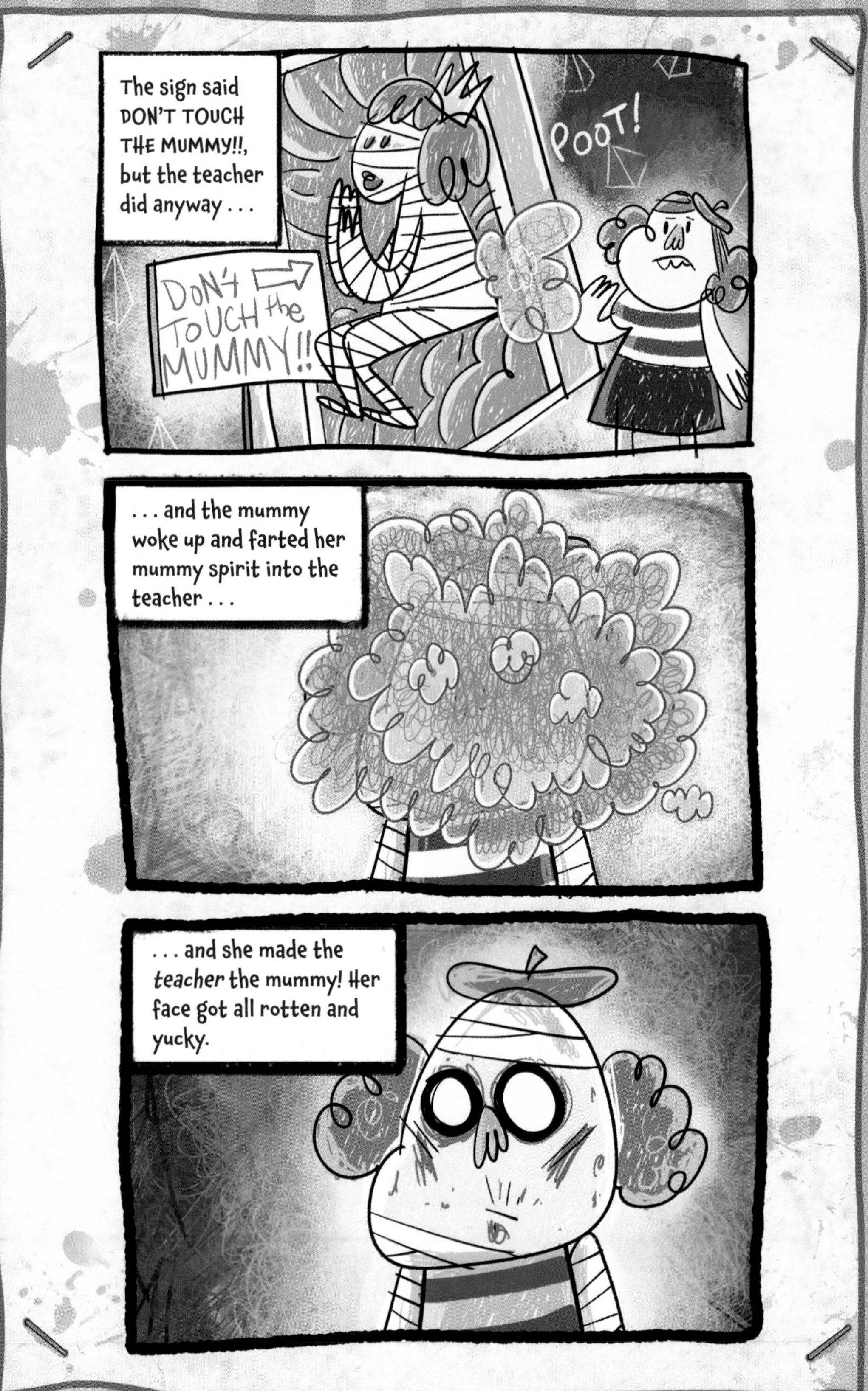
The sign said DON'T TOUCH THE MUMMY!!, but the teacher did anyway . . .
DON'T TOUCH the MUMMY!!
POOT!
. . . and the mummy woke up and farted her mummy spirit into the teacher . . .
. . . and she made the *teacher* the mummy! Her face got all rotten and yucky.

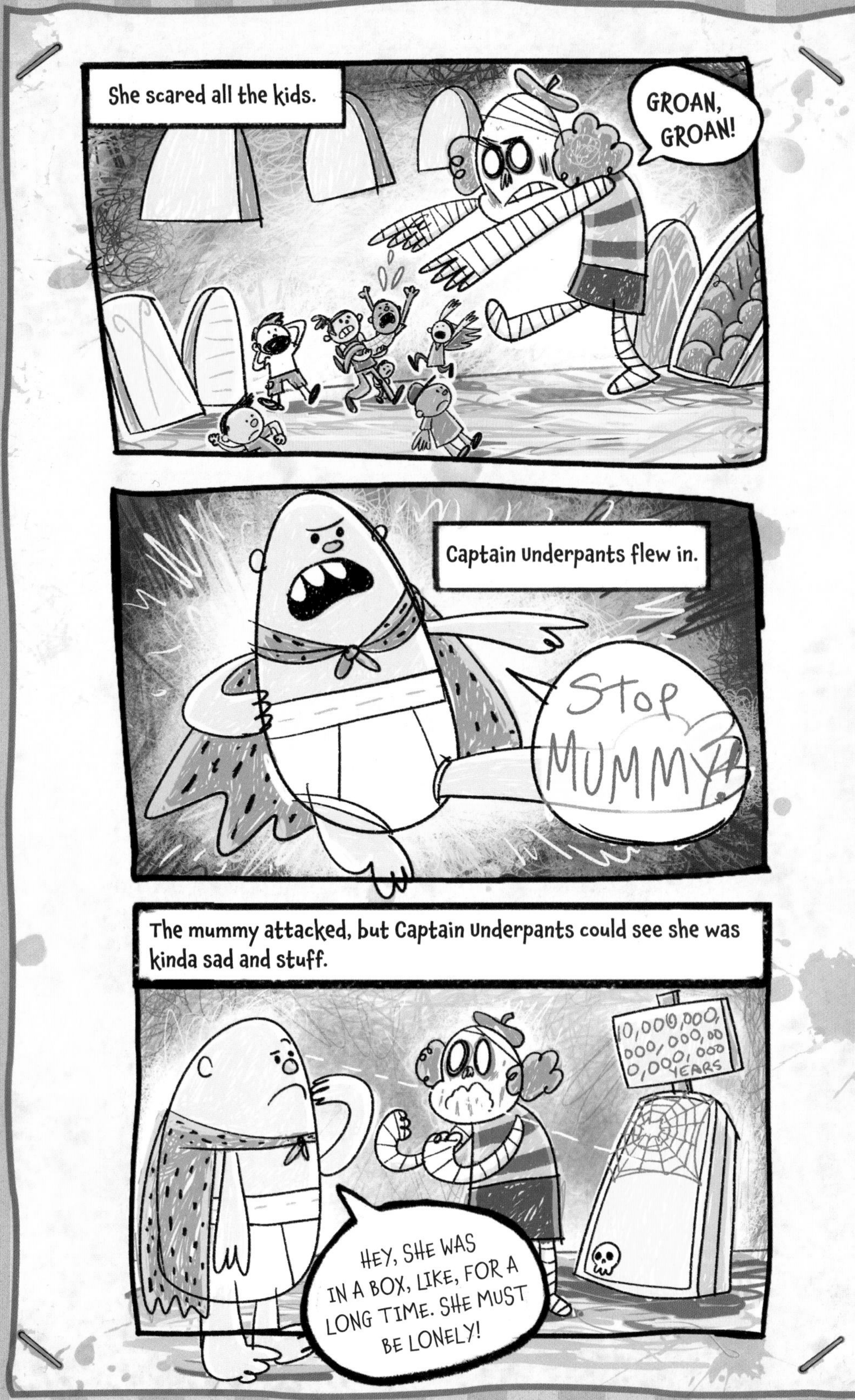
She scared all the kids.
GROAN, GROAN!
Captain Underpants flew in.
STOP MUMMY!
The mummy attacked, but Captain Underpants could see she was kinda sad and stuff.
10,000,000,000,000,000,000,000 YEARS
HEY, SHE WAS IN A BOX, LIKE, FOR A LONG TIME. SHE MUST BE LONELY!

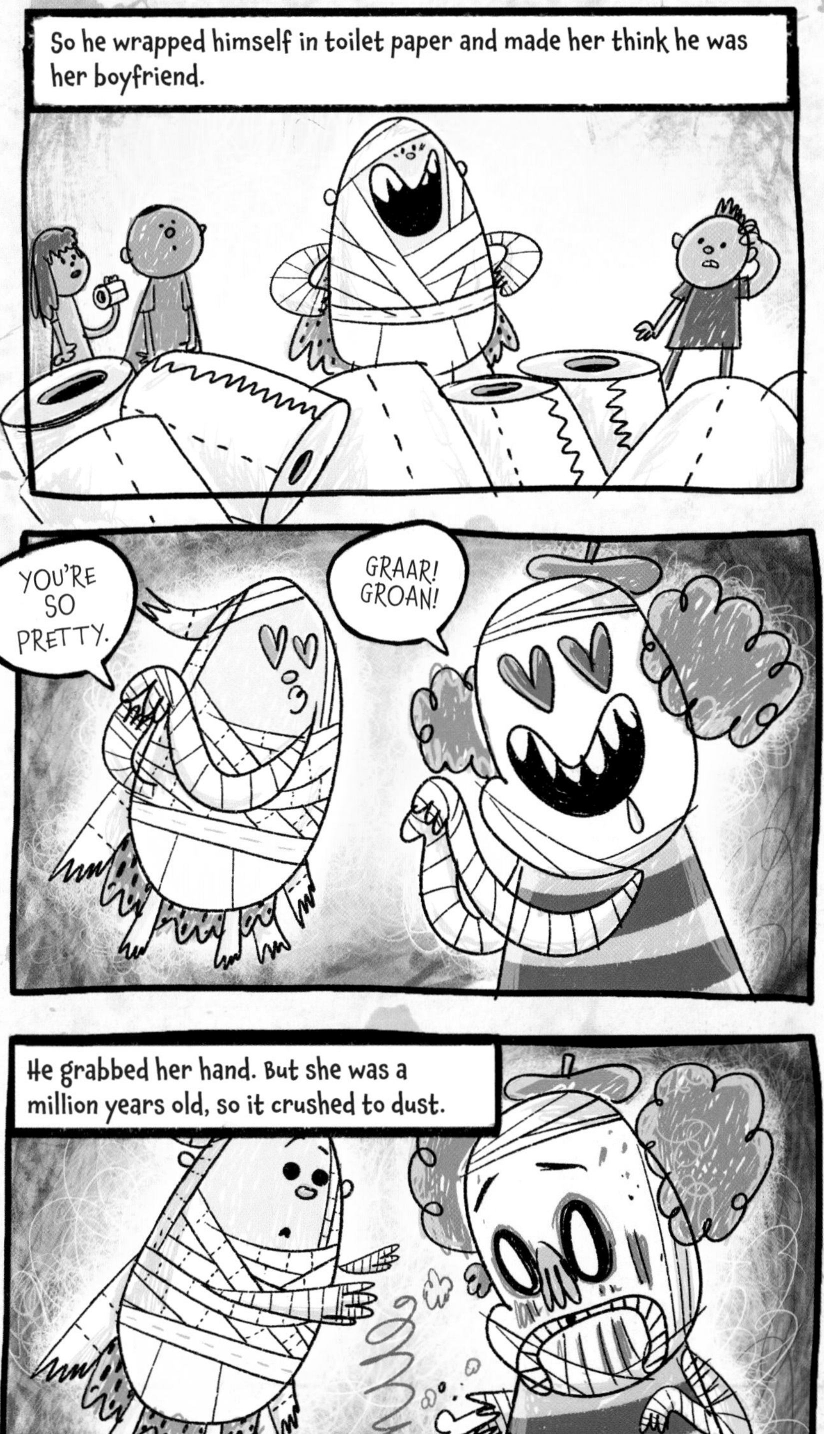
So he wrapped himself in toilet paper and made her think he was her boyfriend.
YOU'RE SO PRETTY.
GRAAR! GROAN!
He grabbed her hand. But she was a million years old, so it crushed to dust.

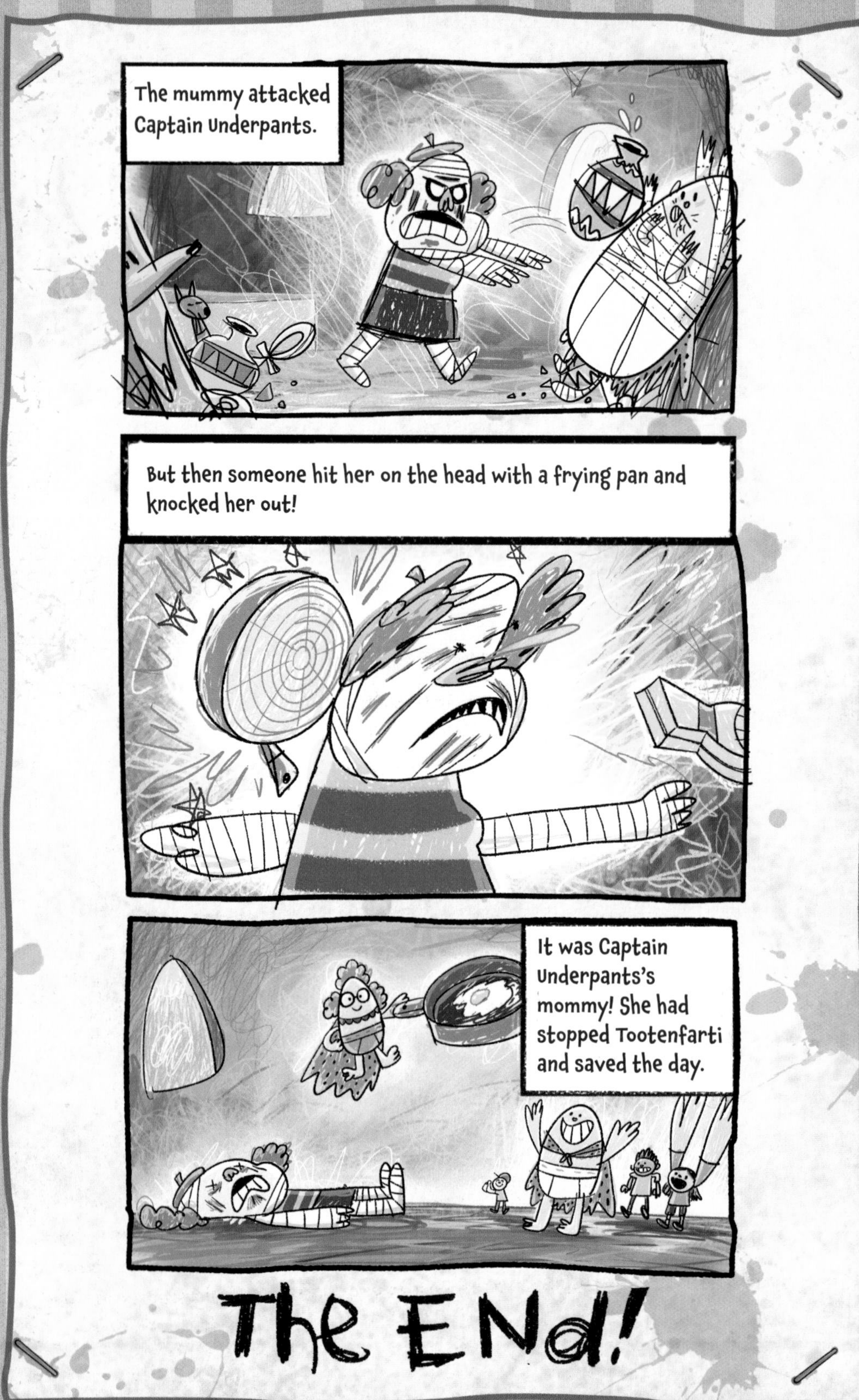
The mummy attacked Captain Underpants.
But then someone hit her on the head with a frying pan and knocked her out!
It was Captain Underpants's mommy! She had stopped Tootenfarti and saved the day.
The End!

The next day at school . . .

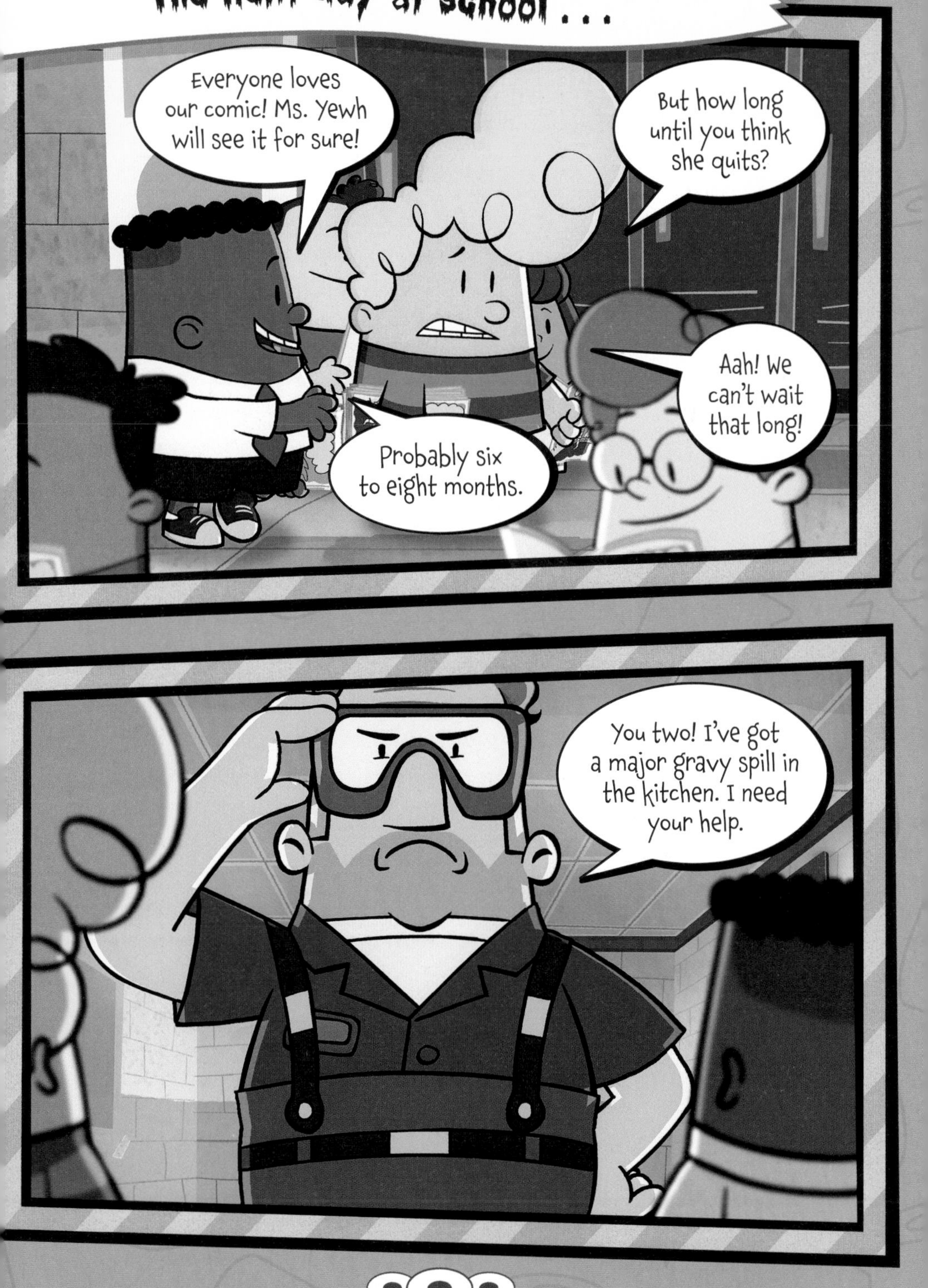
Everyone loves our comic! Ms. Yewh will see it for sure!
But how long until you think she quits?
Probably six to eight months.
Aah! We can't wait that long!
You two! I've got a major gravy spill in the kitchen. I need your help.

You want US to mop up gravy?

Ha! No. You're not certified for that. I need you two to guard that toilet paper.

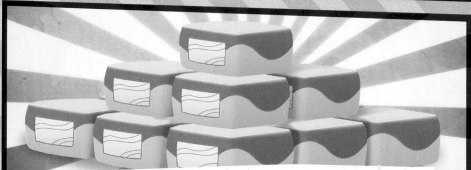

You see, Mr. Krupp had told Mr. Ree to guard the toilet paper, but he didn't say who to guard it from. Which is quite the lucky error for George and Harold and this story.

EEEEEEEEEEEEEEEE!

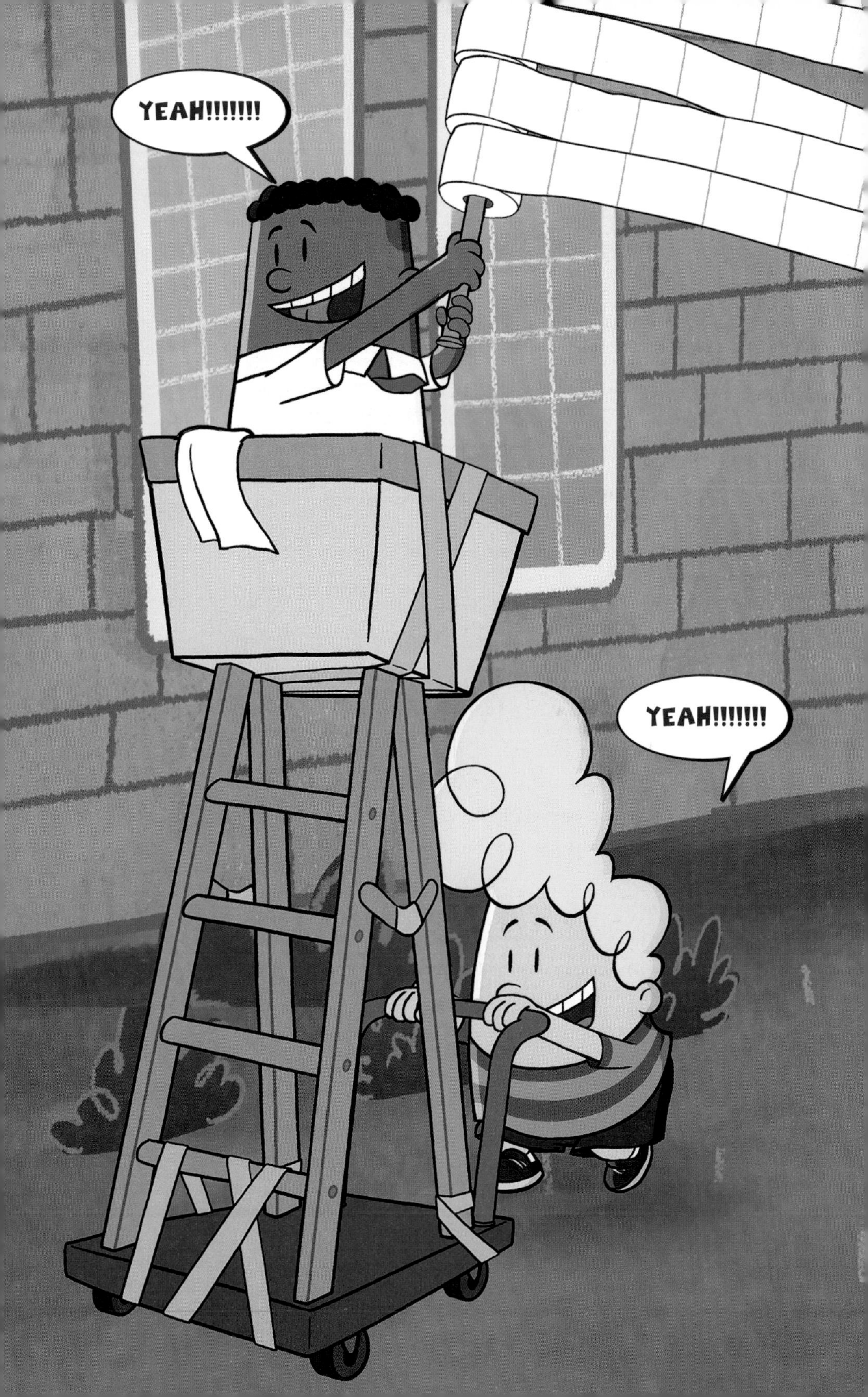
YEAH!!!!!!!
YEAH!!!!!!!

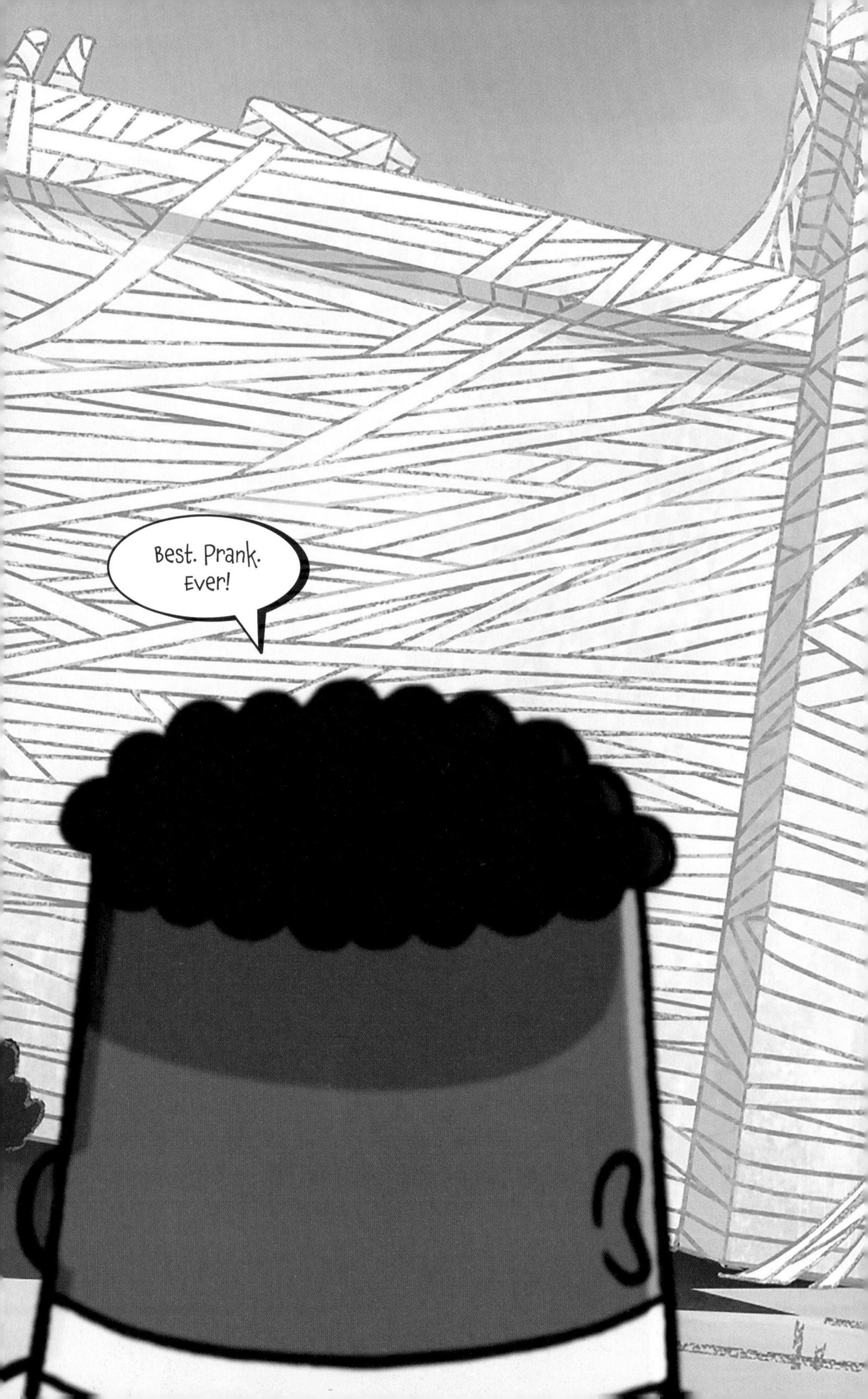
Best. Prank. Ever!

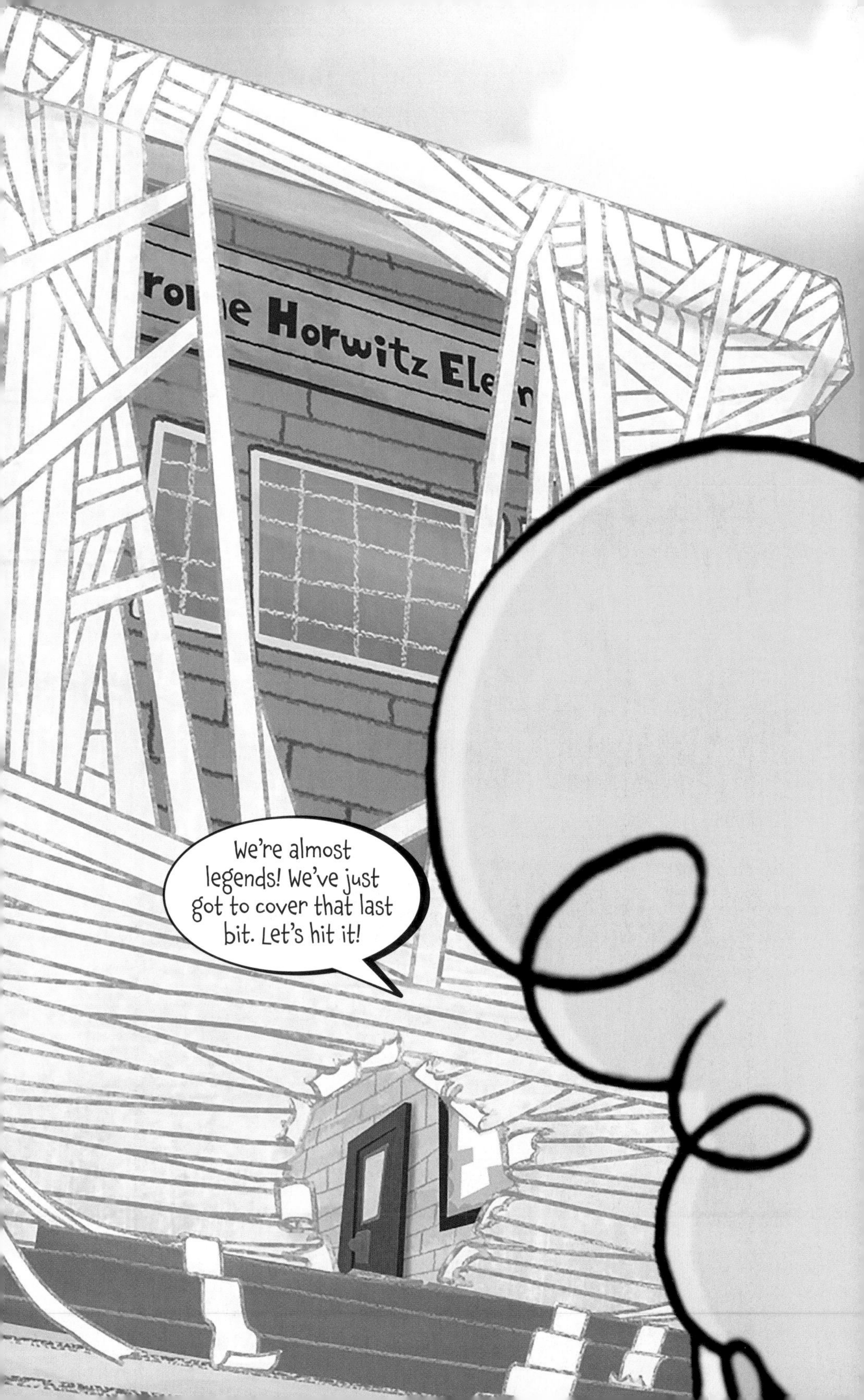
We're almost legends! We've just got to cover that last bit. Let's hit it!

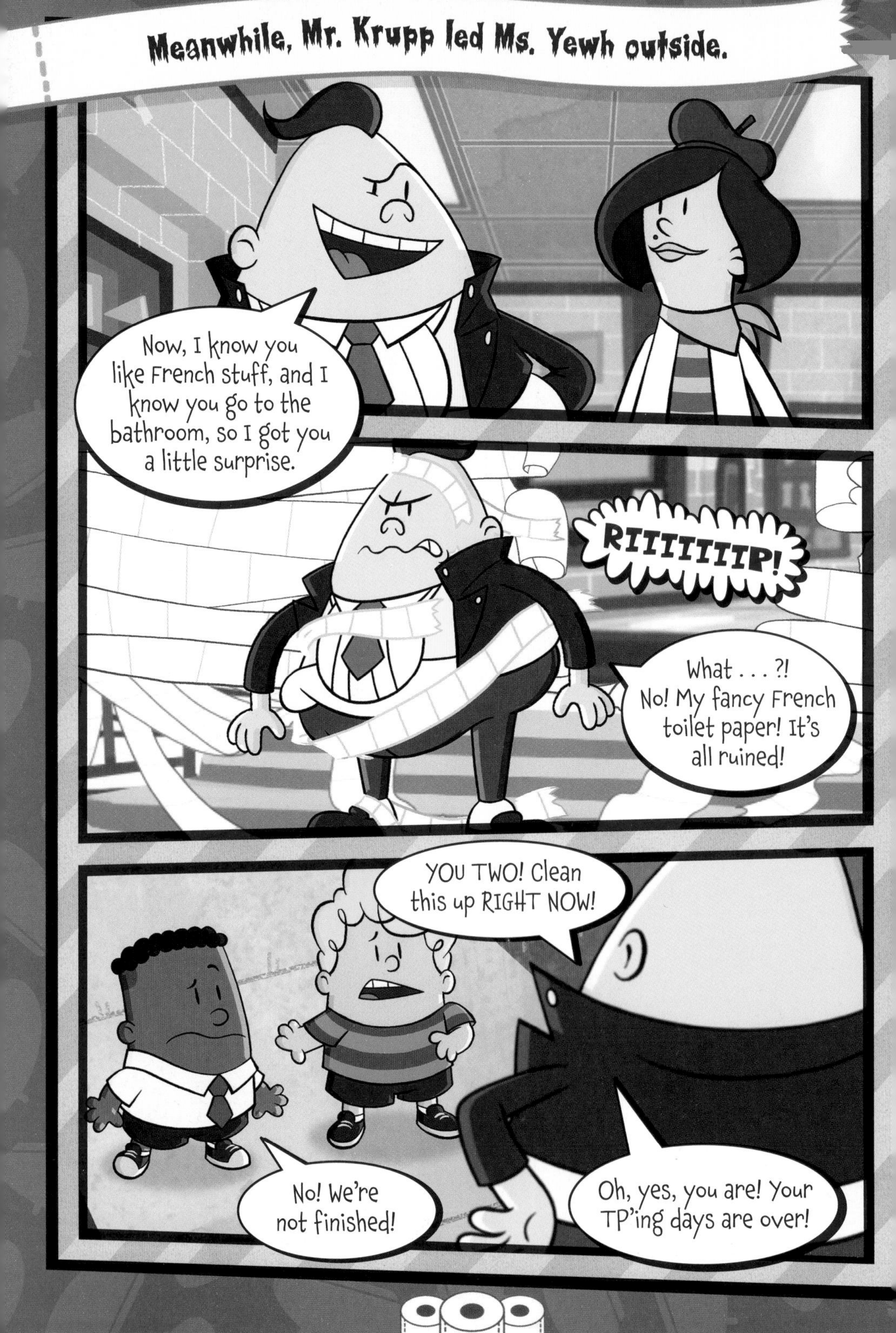
Meanwhile, Mr. Krupp led Ms. Yewh outside.
Now, I know you like French stuff, and I know you go to the bathroom, so I got you a little surprise.
RIIIIIIIP!
What . . . ?! No! My fancy French toilet paper! It's all ruined!
YOU TWO! Clean this up RIGHT NOW!
No! We're not finished!
Oh, yes, you are! Your TP'ing days are over!

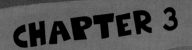

CHAPTER 3

ROYAL FLUSH

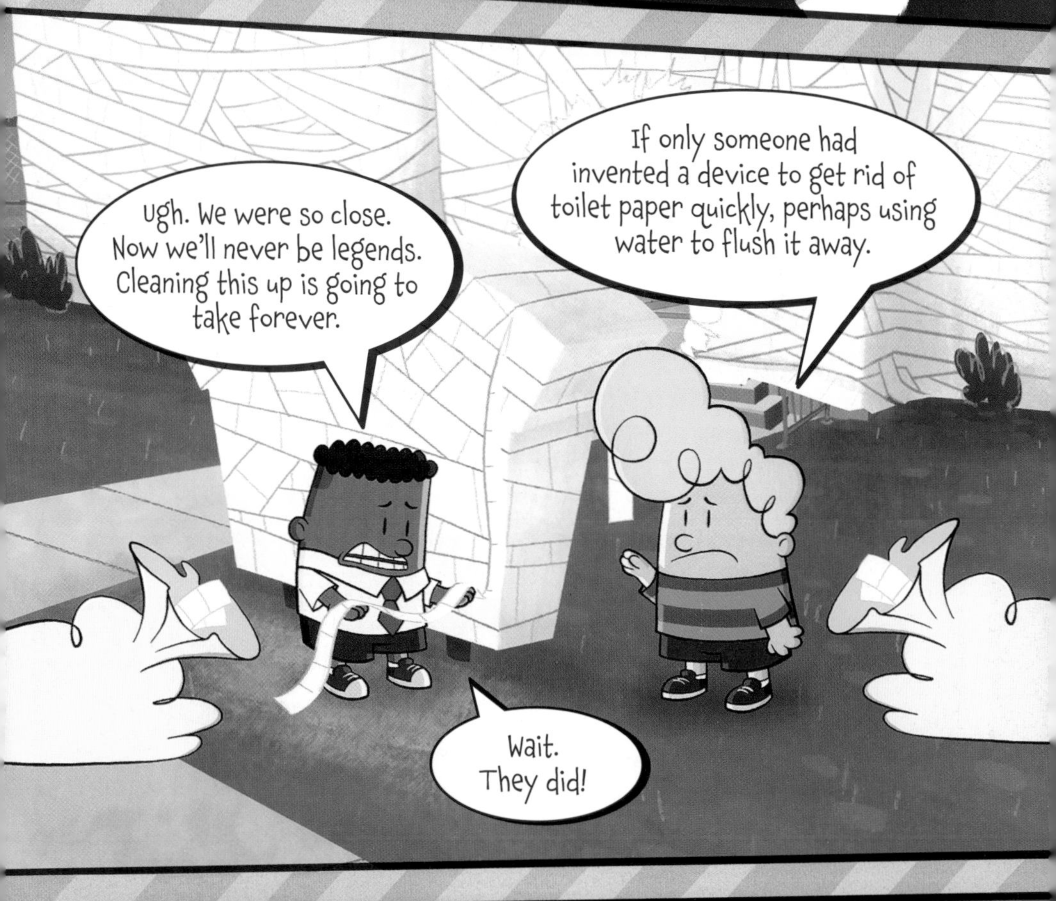
Ugh. We were so close. Now we'll never be legends. Cleaning this up is going to take forever.
If only someone had invented a device to get rid of toilet paper quickly, perhaps using water to flush it away.
Wait. They did!

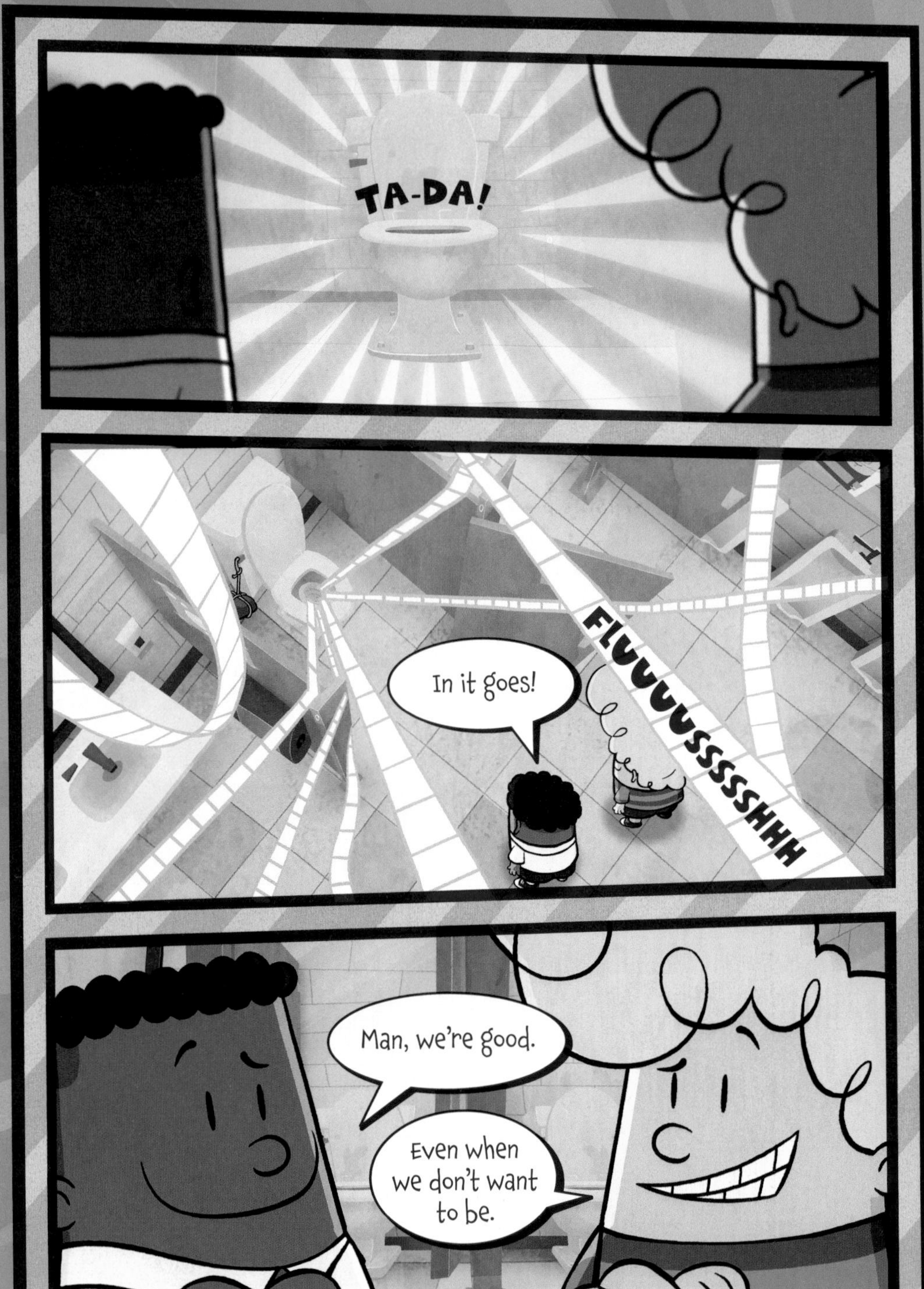
TA-DA!
In it goes!
FLUUUUSSSSSSHHH
Man, we're good.
Even when we don't want to be.

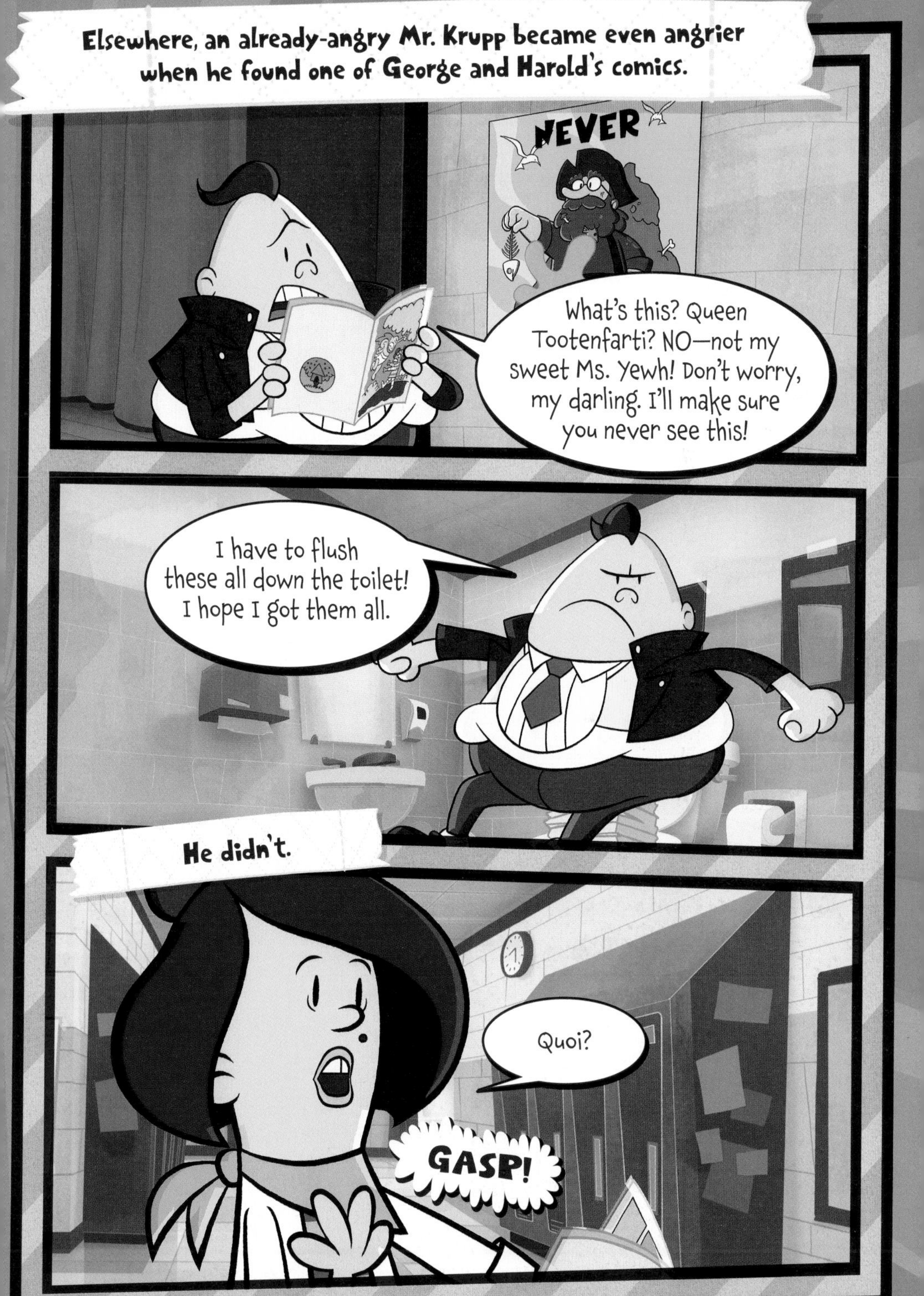
Elsewhere, an already-angry Mr. Krupp became even angrier when he found one of George and Harold's comics.
NEVER
What's this? Queen Tootenfarti? NO—not my sweet Ms. Yewh! Don't worry, my darling. I'll make sure you never see this!
I have to flush these all down the toilet! I hope I got them all.
He didn't.
Quoi?
GASP!

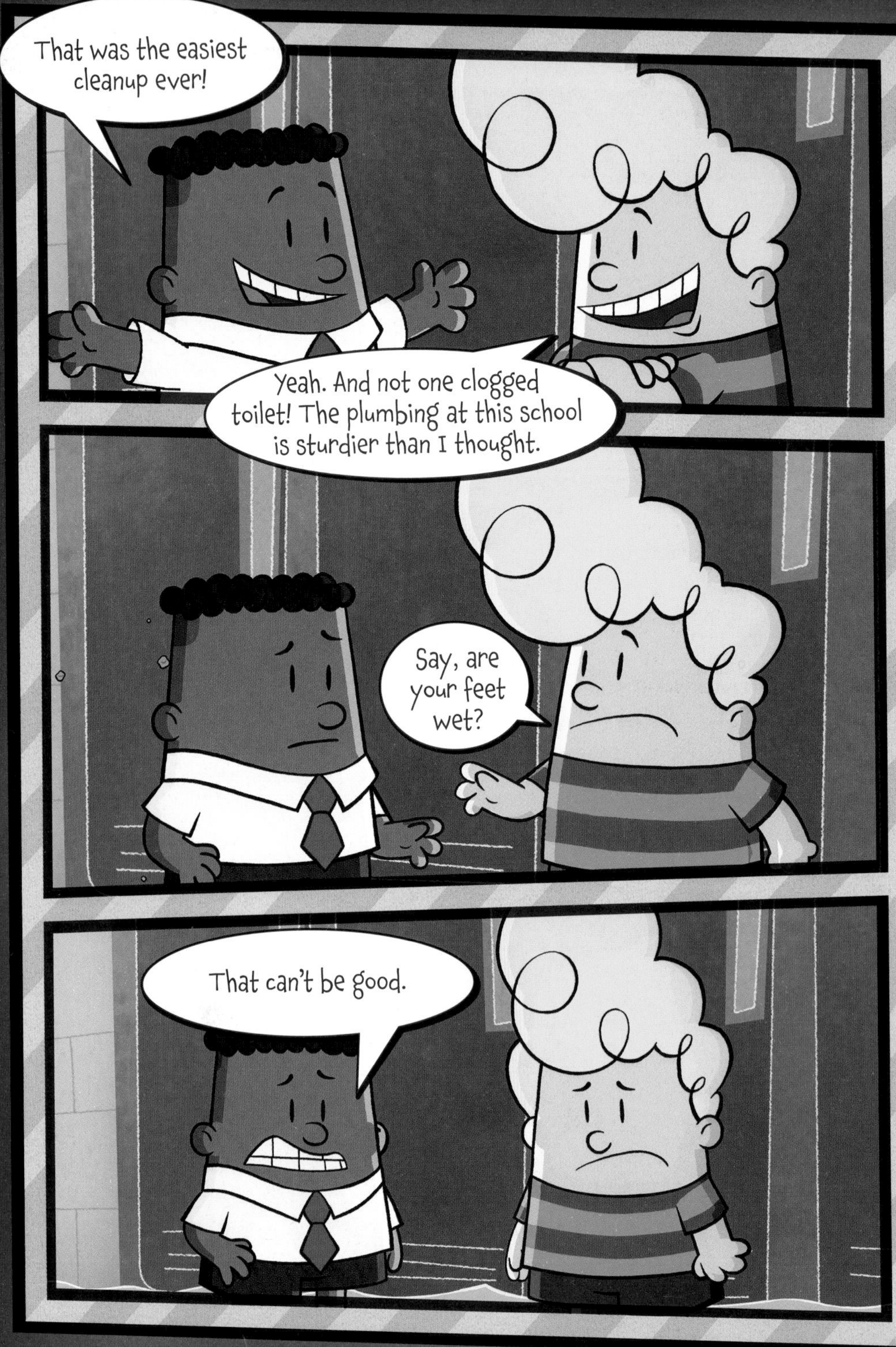
That was the easiest cleanup ever!
Yeah. And not one clogged toilet! The plumbing at this school is sturdier than I thought.
Say, are your feet wet?
That can't be good.

CHAPTER 4

NO IT CAN'T

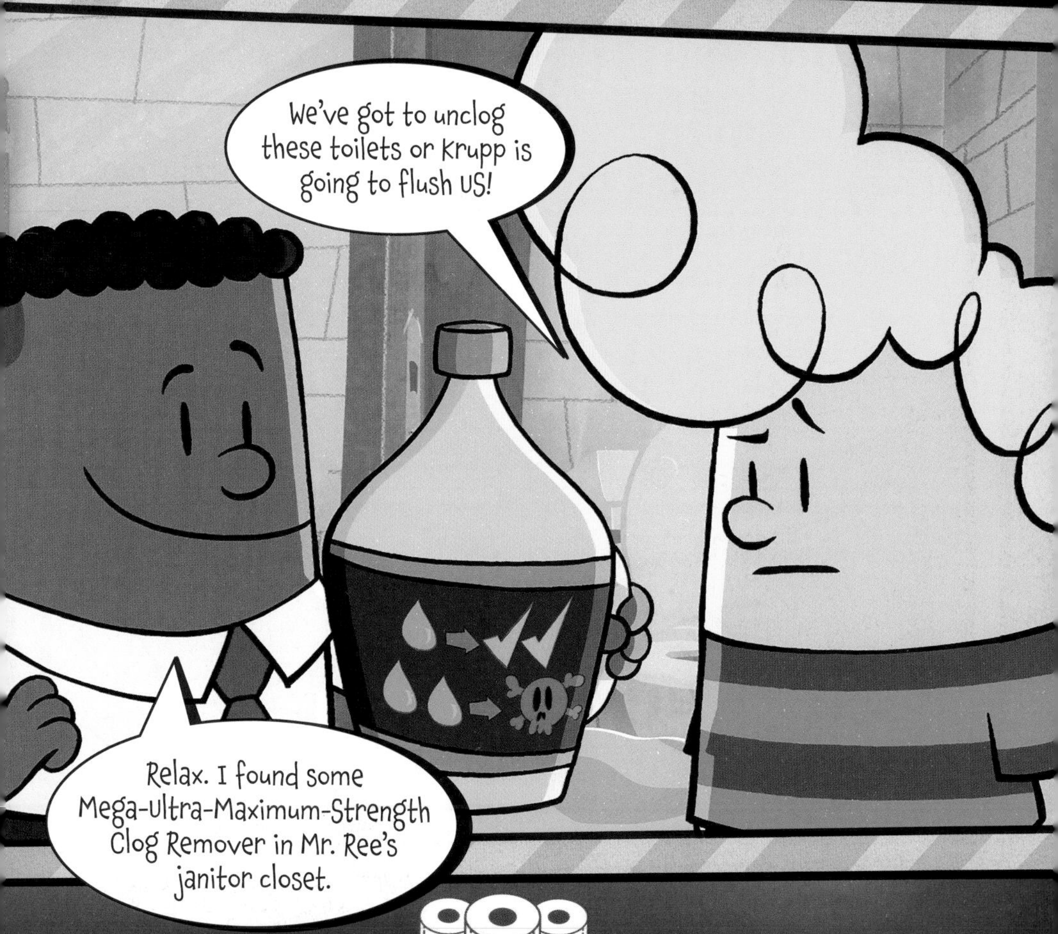
We've got to unclog these toilets or Krupp is going to flush US!
Relax. I found some Mega-Ultra-Maximum-Strength Clog Remover in Mr. Ree's janitor closet.

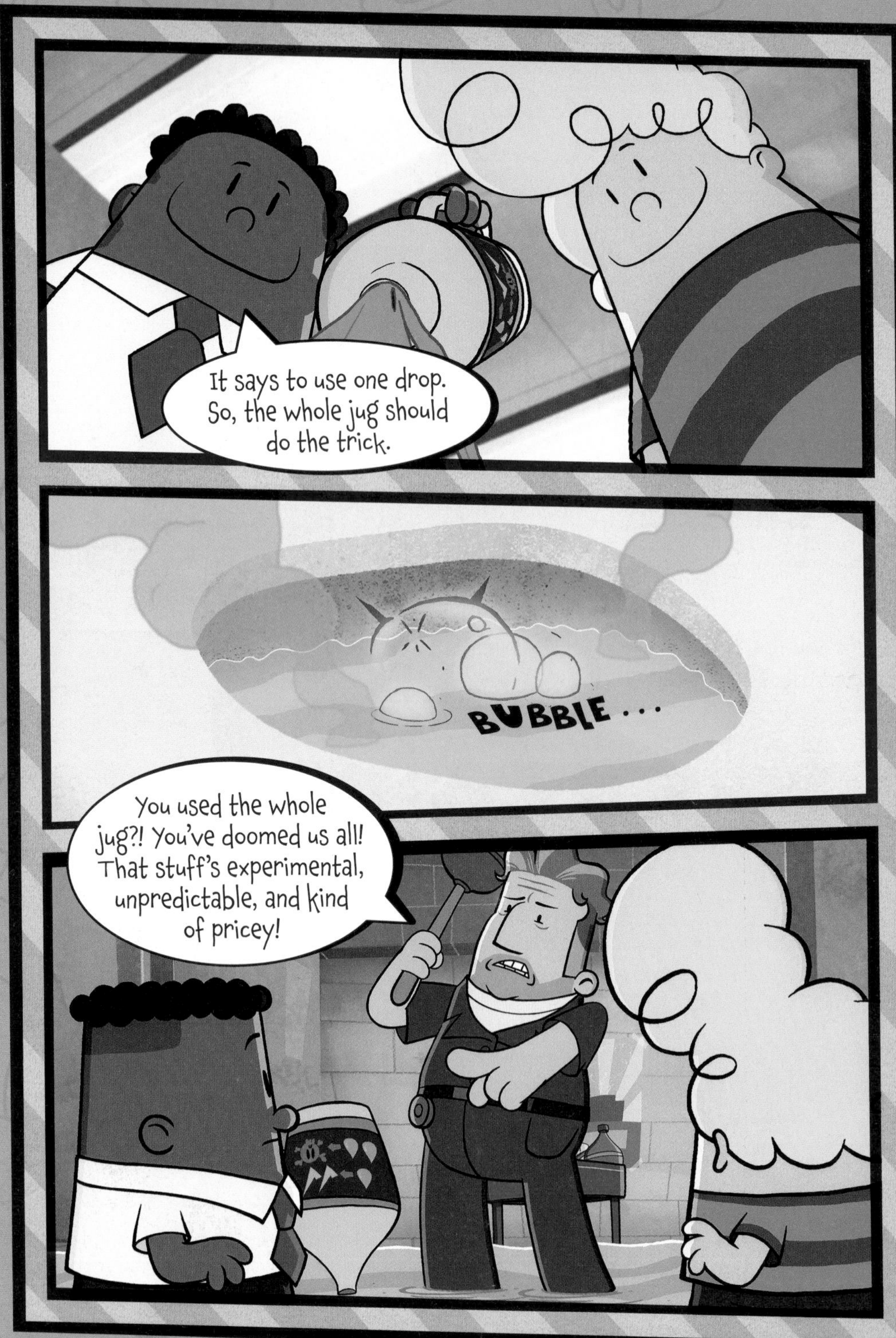
It says to use one drop. So, the whole jug should do the trick.
BUBBLE . . .
You used the whole jug?! You've doomed us all! That stuff's experimental, unpredictable, and kind of pricey!

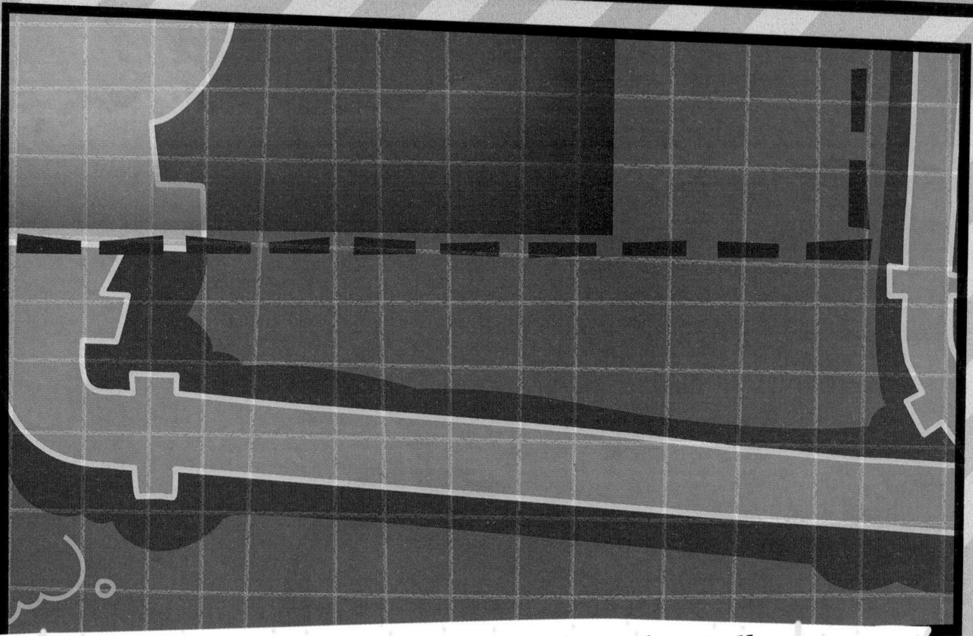

Now, it's a little-known fact that the pipes at Jerome Horwitz are rated to handle the flushing of exactly 47 comics, one gallon of de-clogger, and 500 rolls of toilet paper. As long as no one flushed one more . . .

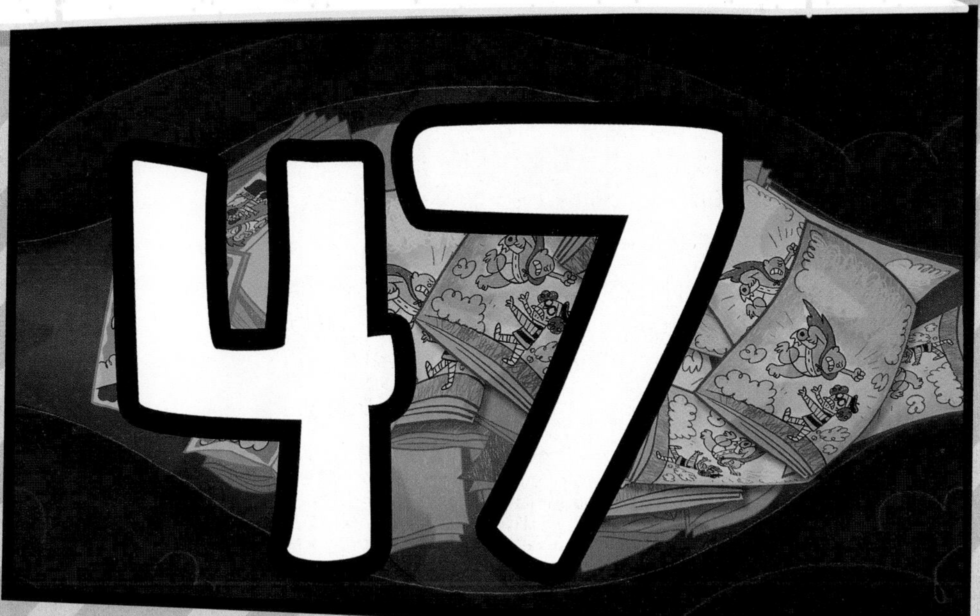
47

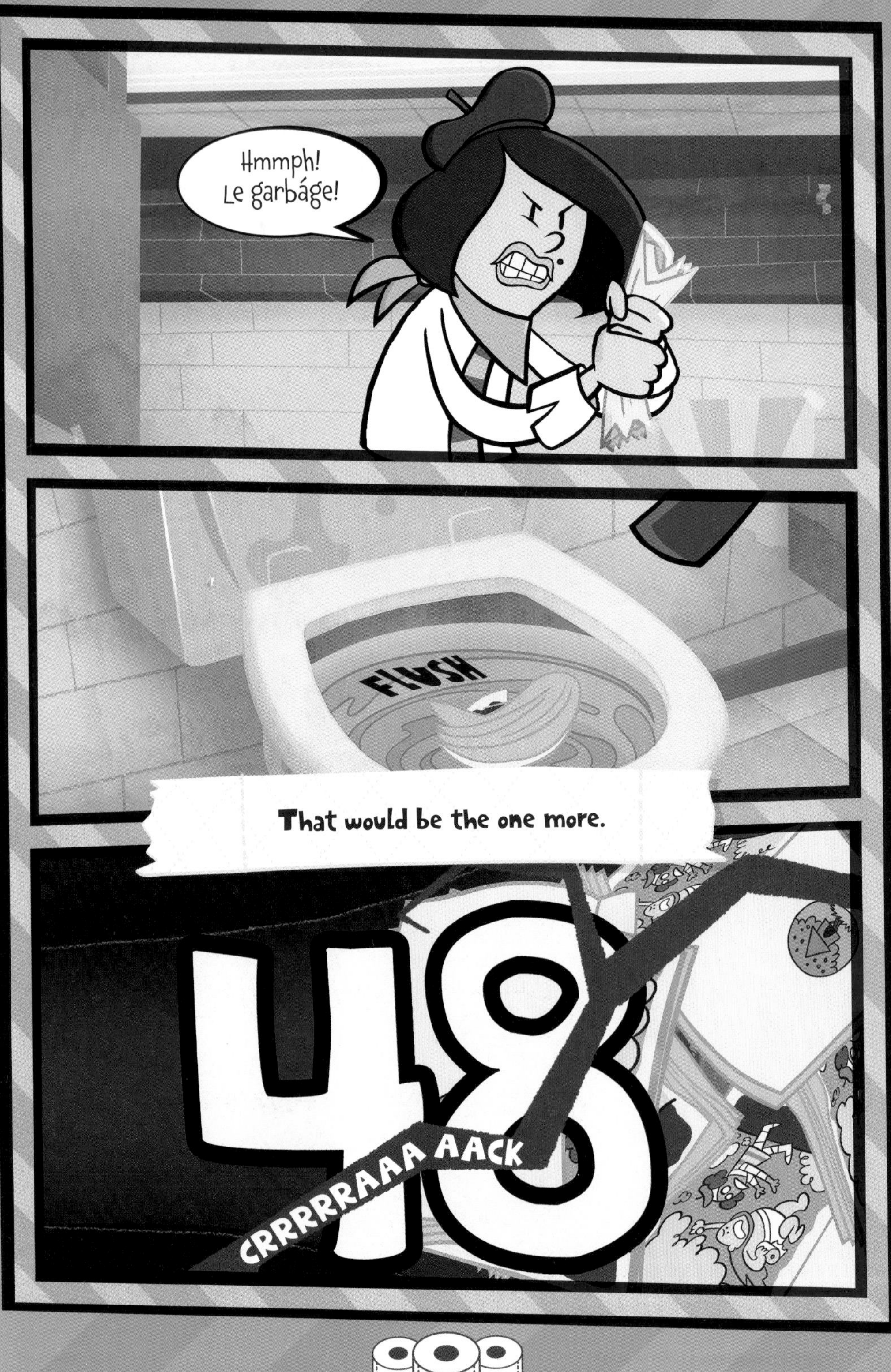
Hmmph! Le garbáge!
FLUSH
That would be the one more.
48
CRRRRRAAA AACK

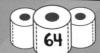

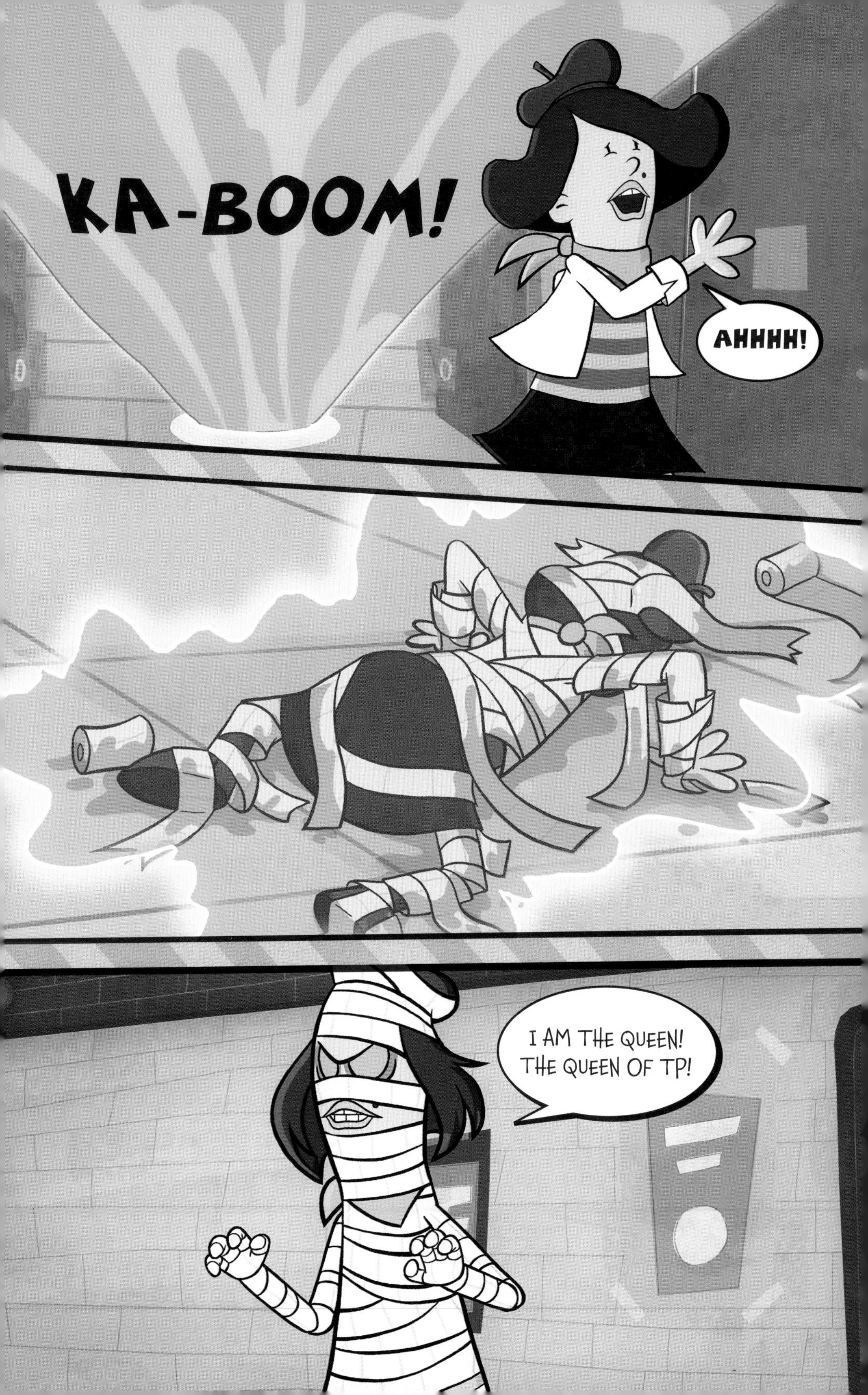
KA-BOOM!
AHHHH!
I AM THE QUEEN! THE QUEEN OF TP!

CHAPTER 5

SPEED HATING

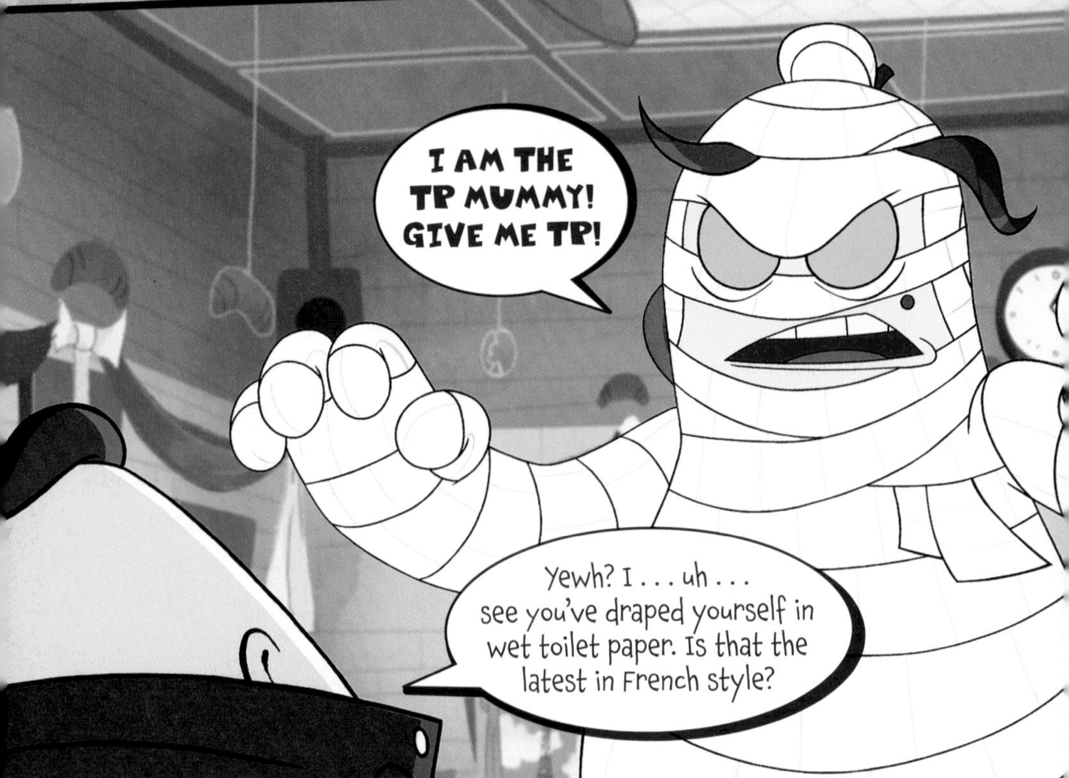
I AM THE TP MUMMY! GIVE ME TP!
Yewh? I . . . uh . . . see you've draped yourself in wet toilet paper. Is that the latest in French style?

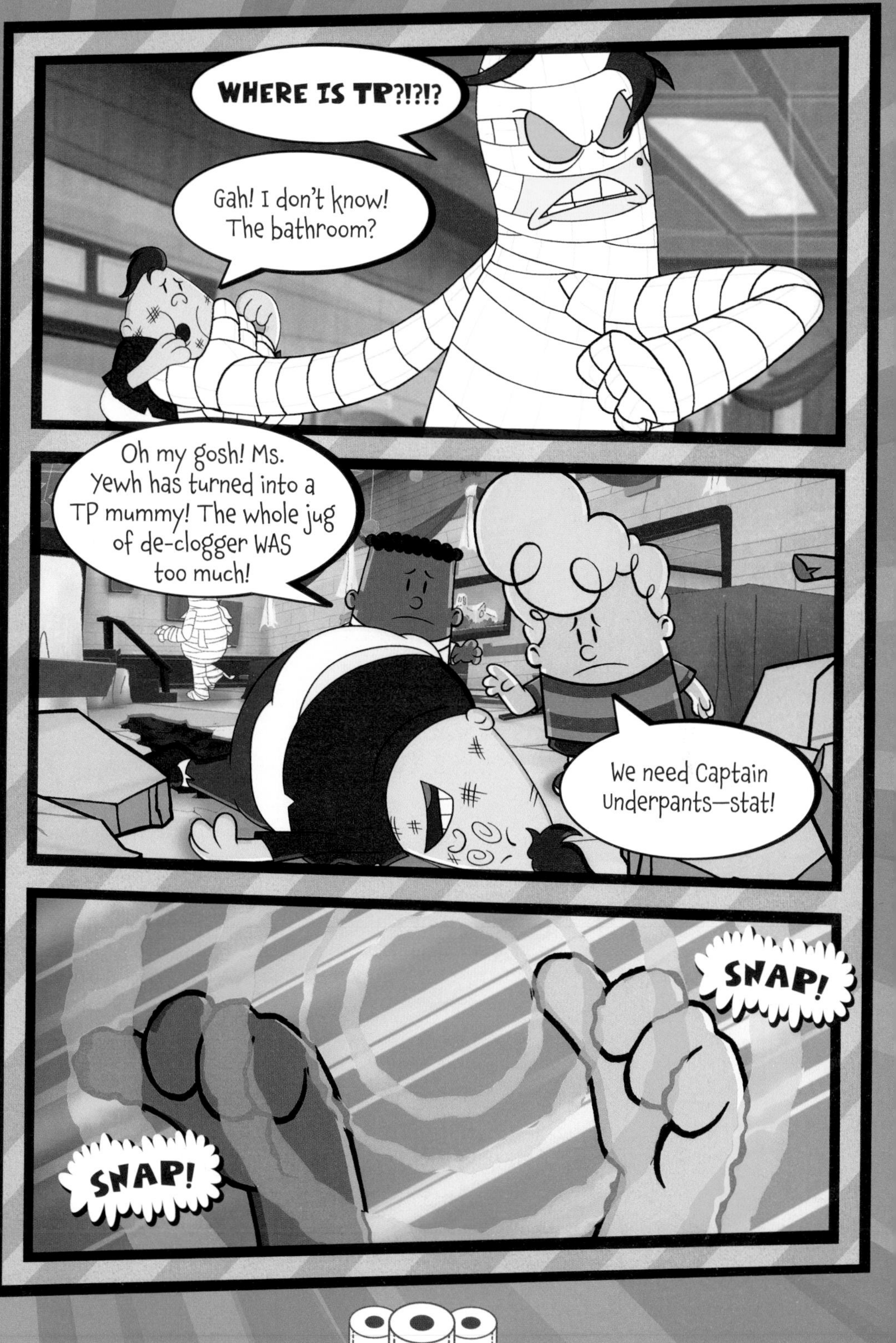
WHERE IS TP?!?!?
Gah! I don't know! The bathroom?
Oh my gosh! Ms. Yewh has turned into a TP mummy! The whole jug of de-clogger WAS too much!
We need Captain Underpants—stat!
SNAP!
SNAP!

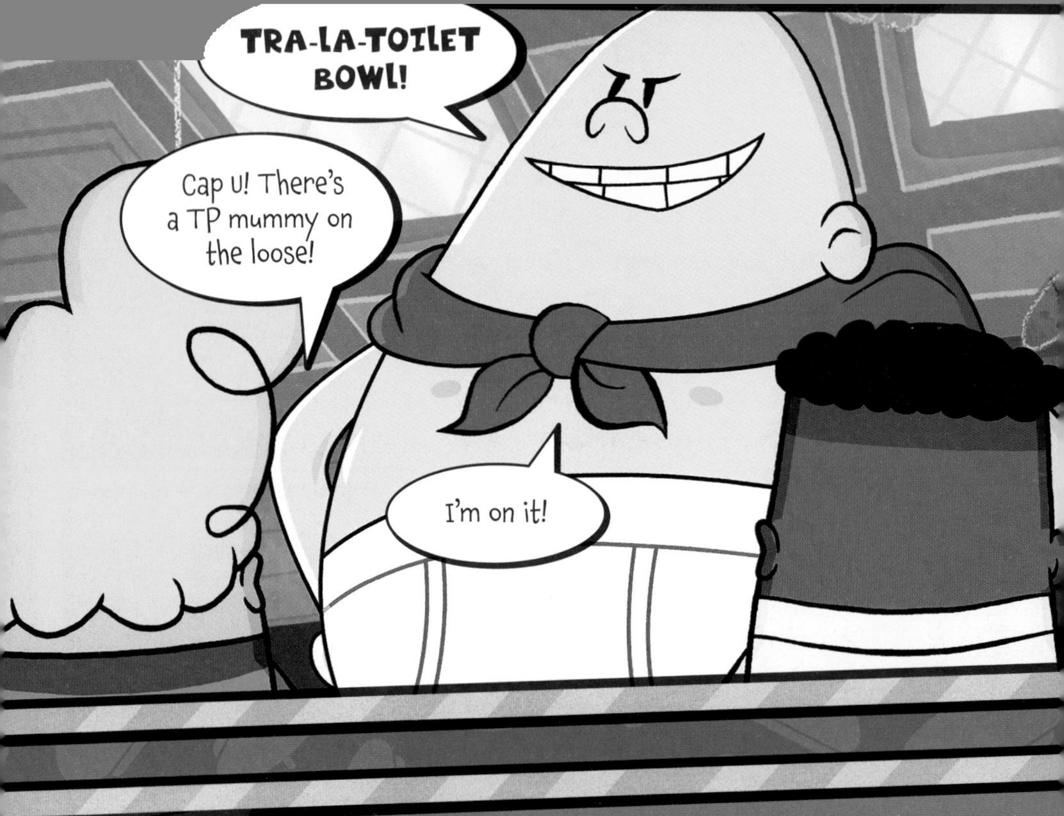
TRA-LA-TOILET BOWL!
Cap U! There's a TP mummy on the loose!
I'm on it!

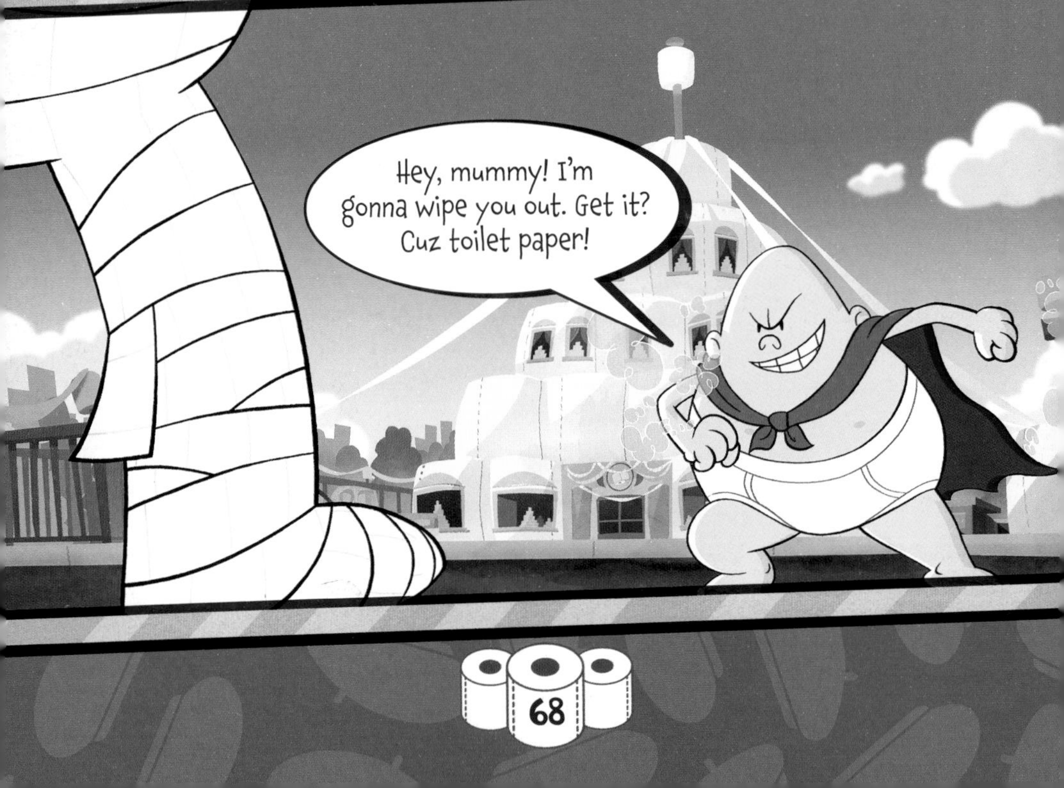
Hey, mummy! I'm gonna wipe you out. Get it? Cuz toilet paper!

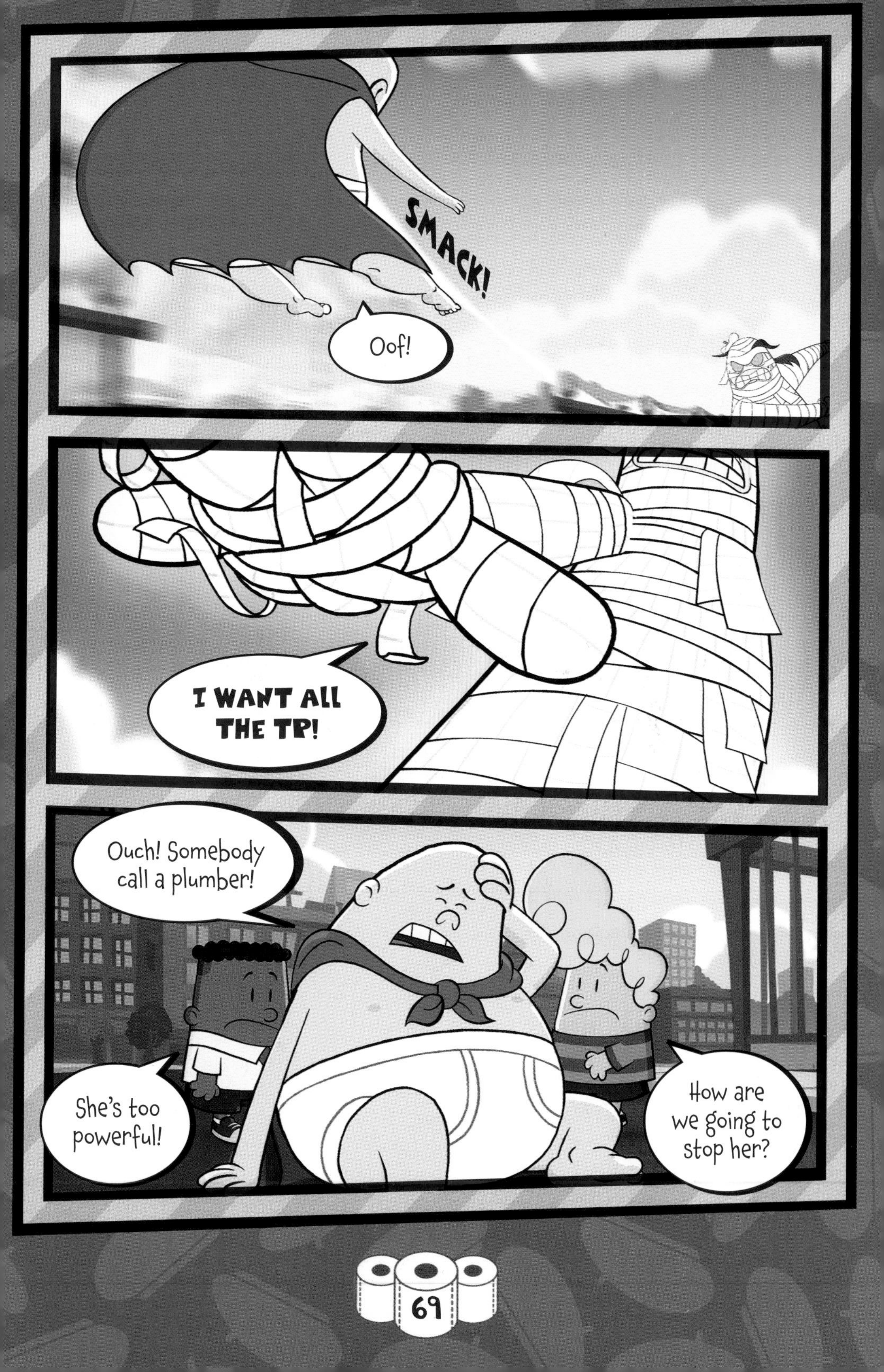
SMACK!
Oof!
I WANT ALL THE TP!
Ouch! Somebody call a plumber!
She's too powerful!
How are we going to stop her?

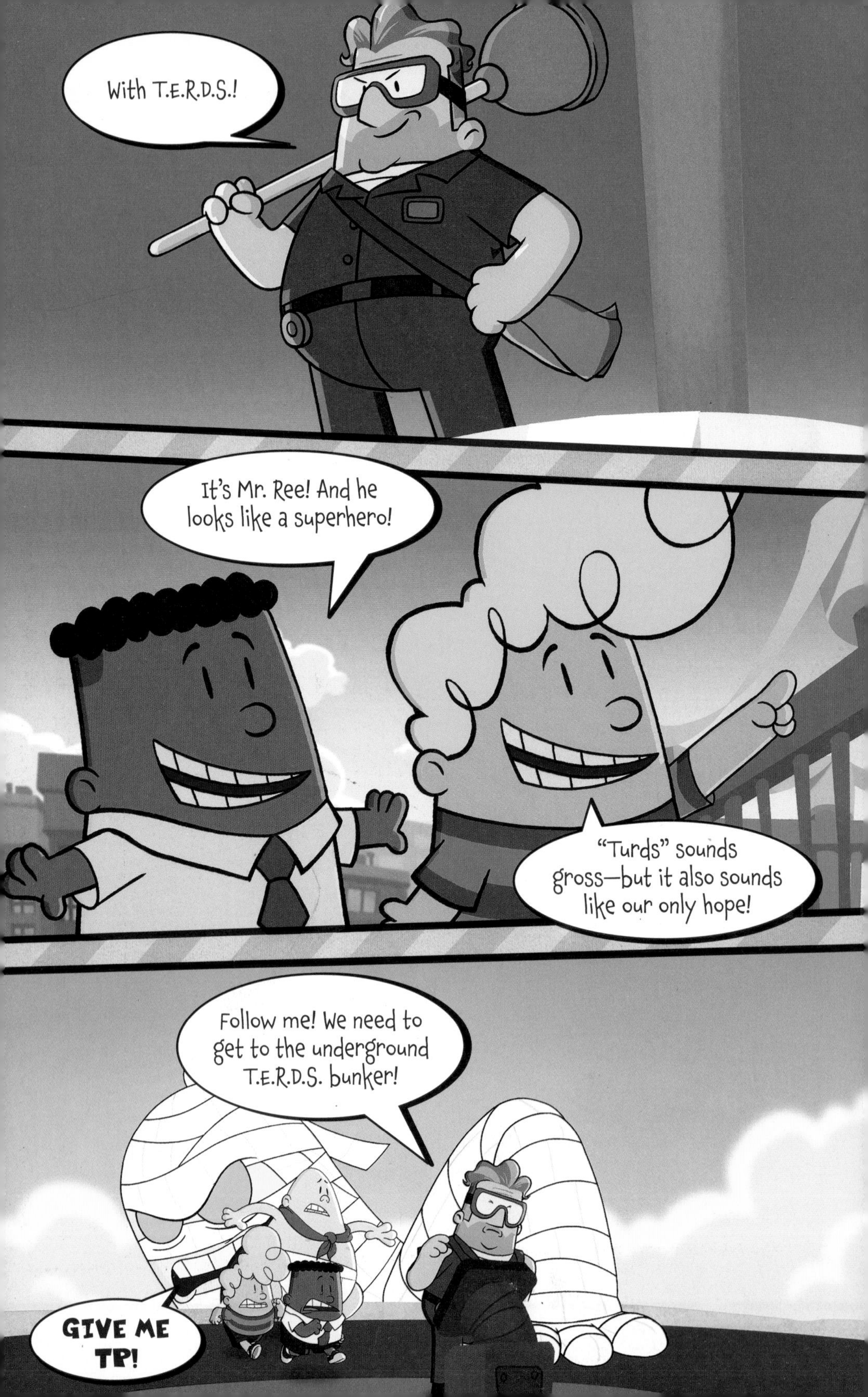
With T.E.R.D.S.!
It's Mr. Ree! And he looks like a superhero!
"Turds" sounds gross—but it also sounds like our only hope!
Follow me! We need to get to the underground T.E.R.D.S. bunker!
GIVE ME TP!

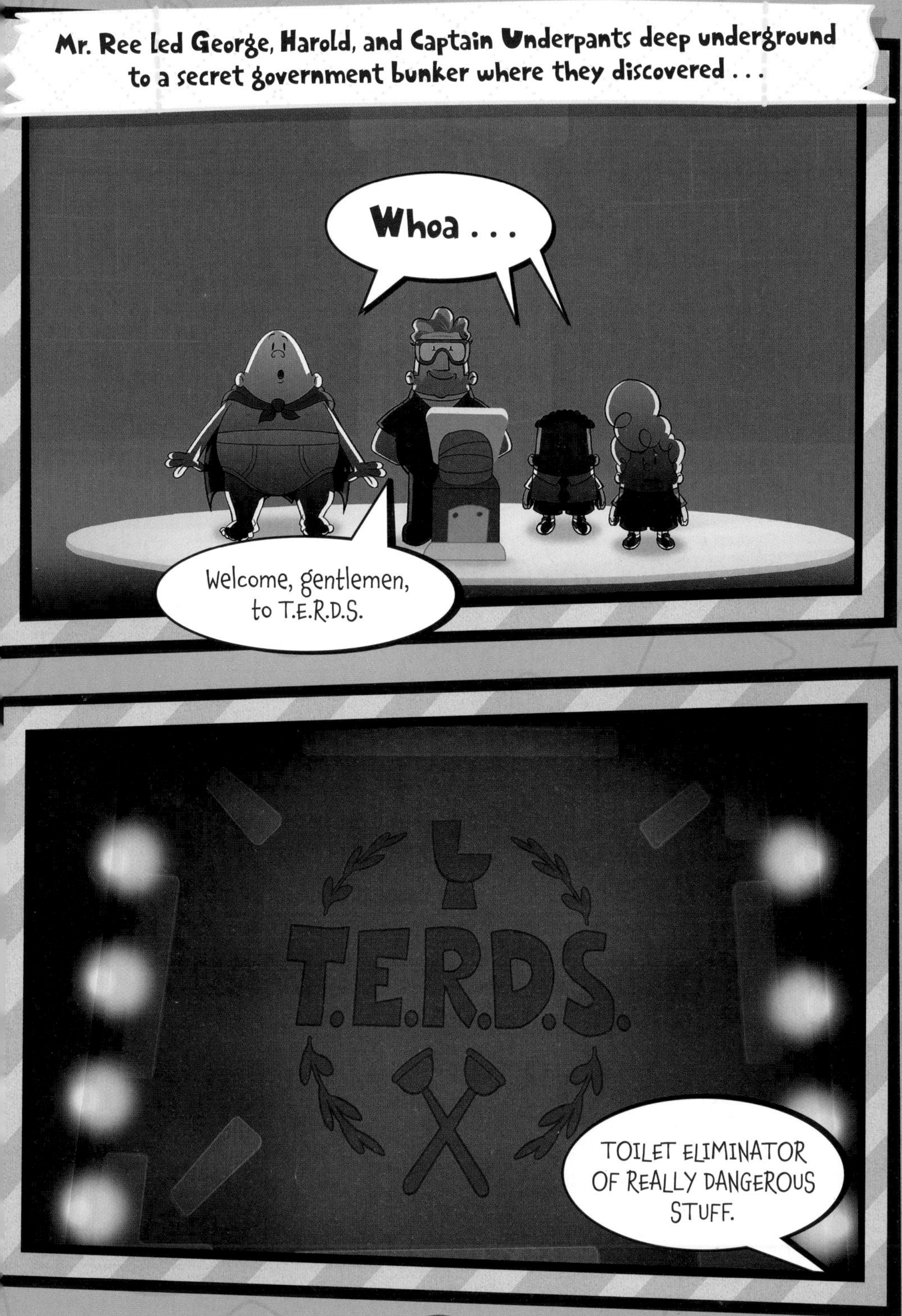
Mr. Ree led George, Harold, and Captain Underpants deep underground to a secret government bunker where they discovered . . .
Whoa . . .
Welcome, gentlemen, to T.E.R.D.S.
T.E.R.D.S.
TOILET ELIMINATOR OF REALLY DANGEROUS STUFF.

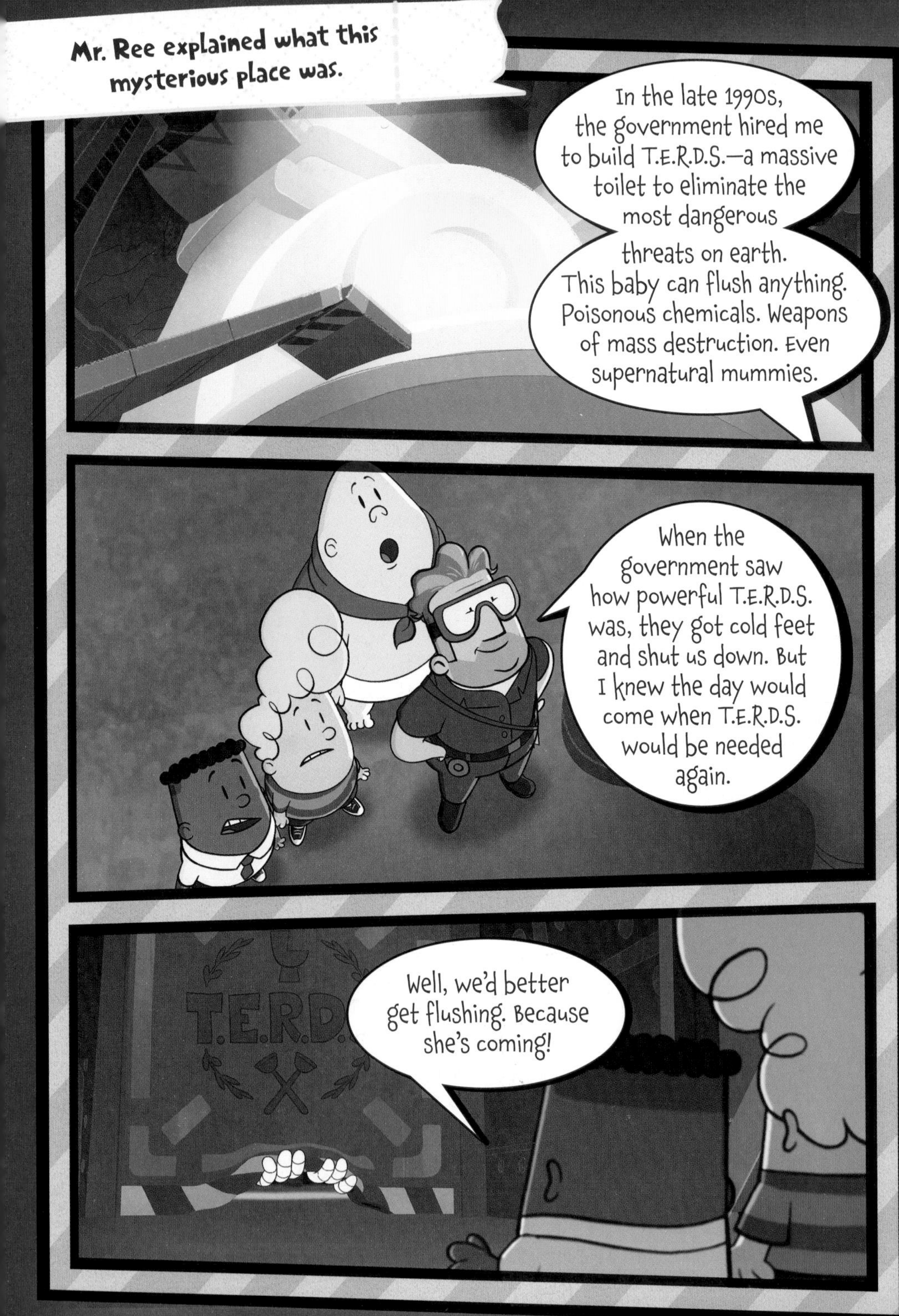
Mr. Ree explained what this mysterious place was.
In the late 1990s, the government hired me to build T.E.R.D.S.—a massive toilet to eliminate the most dangerous threats on earth. This baby can flush anything. Poisonous chemicals. Weapons of mass destruction. Even supernatural mummies.
When the government saw how powerful T.E.R.D.S. was, they got cold feet and shut us down. But I knew the day would come when T.E.R.D.S. would be needed again.
T.E.R.D.
Well, we'd better get flushing. Because she's coming!

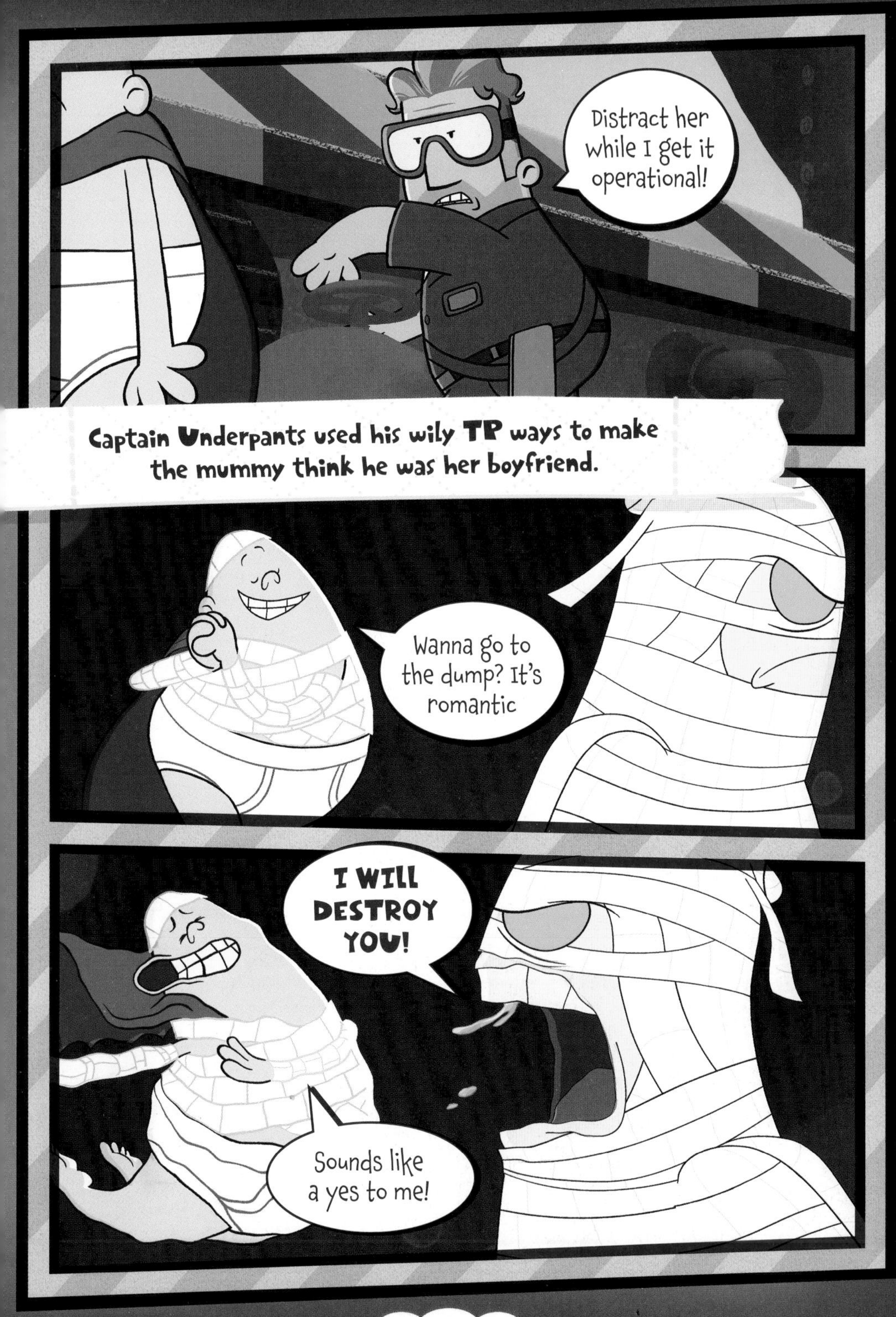
Distract her while I get it operational!
Captain Underpants used his wily TP ways to make the mummy think he was her boyfriend.
Wanna go to the dump? It's romantic
I WILL DESTROY YOU!
Sounds like a yes to me!

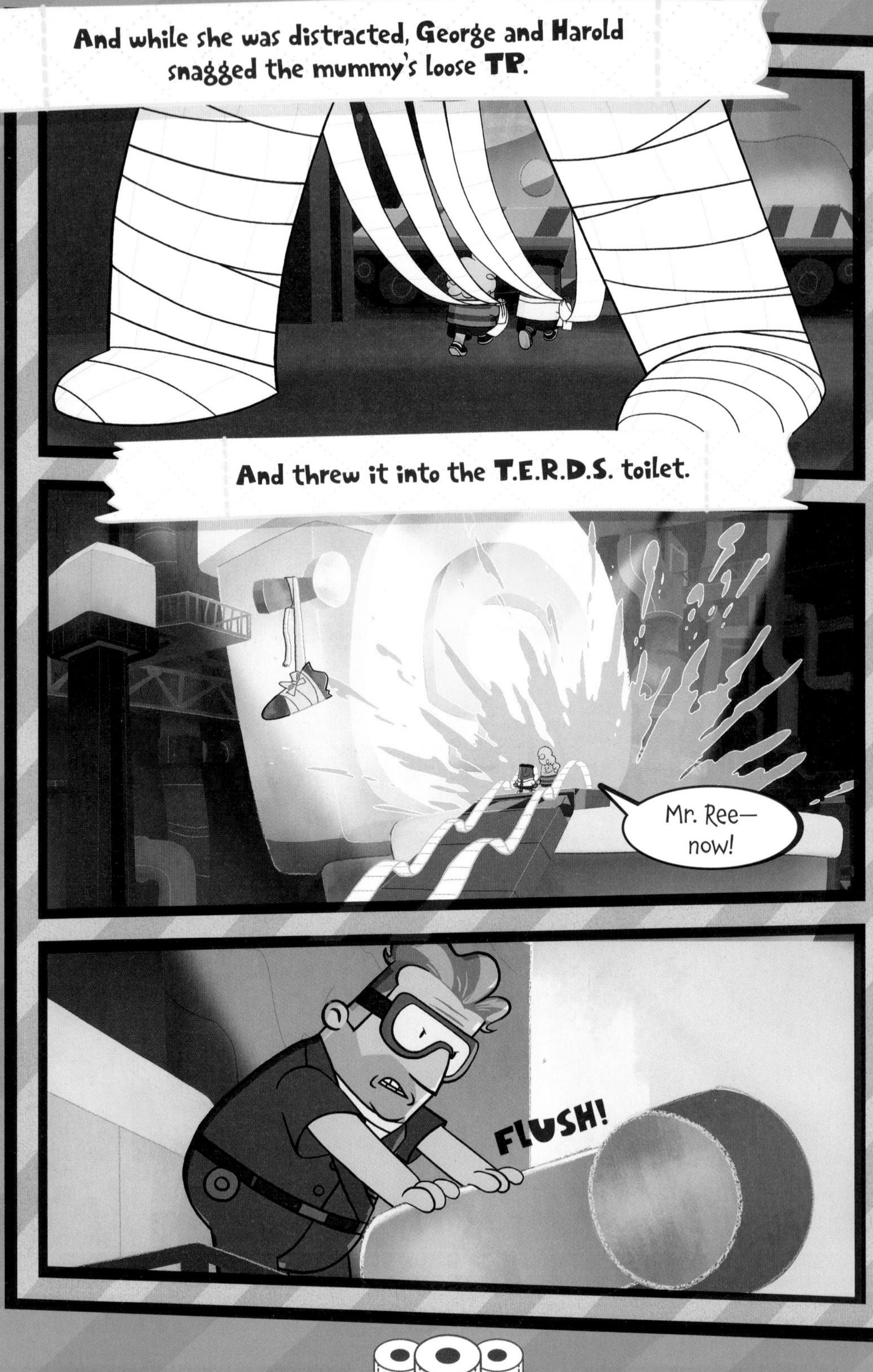
And while she was distracted, George and Harold snagged the mummy's loose TP.
And threw it into the T.E.R.D.S. toilet.
Mr. Ree—now!
FLUSH!

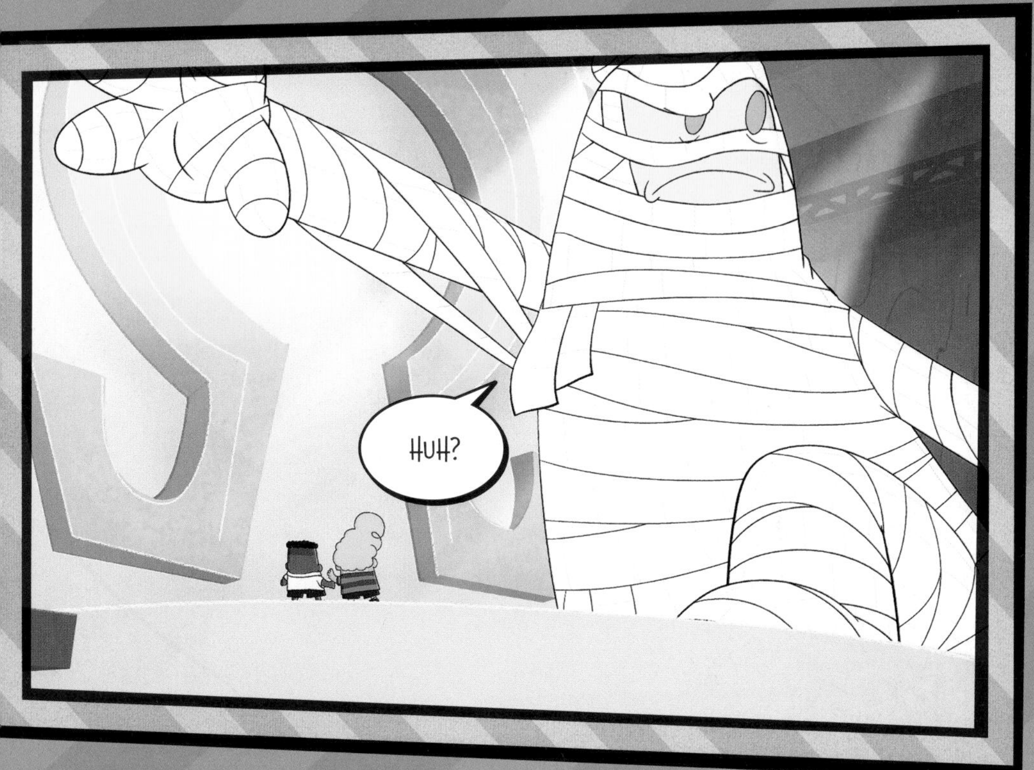
HUH?

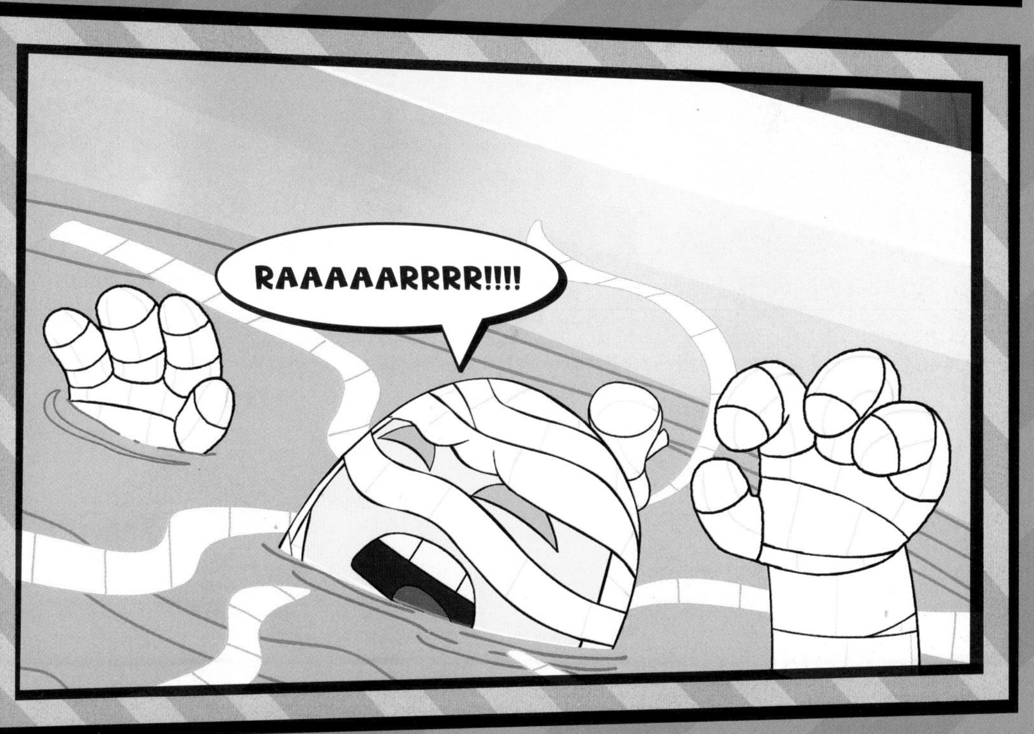
RAAAAARRRR!!!!

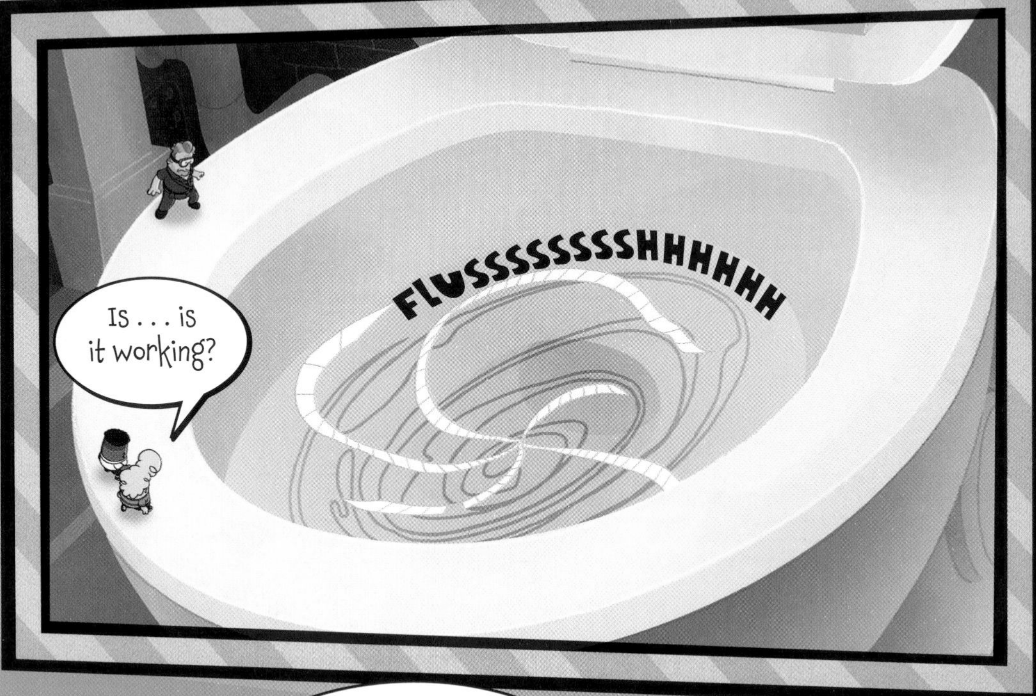
FLUSSSSSSSSHHHHHH
Is . . . is it working?

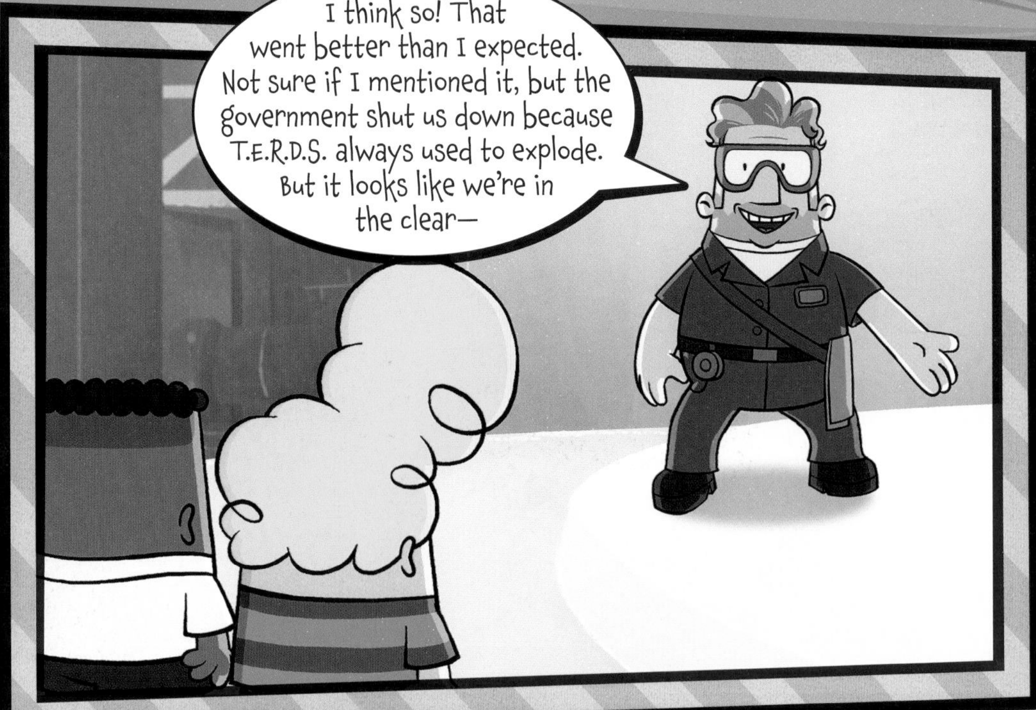
I think so! That went better than I expected. Not sure if I mentioned it, but the government shut us down because T.E.R.D.S. always used to explode. But it looks like we're in the clear—

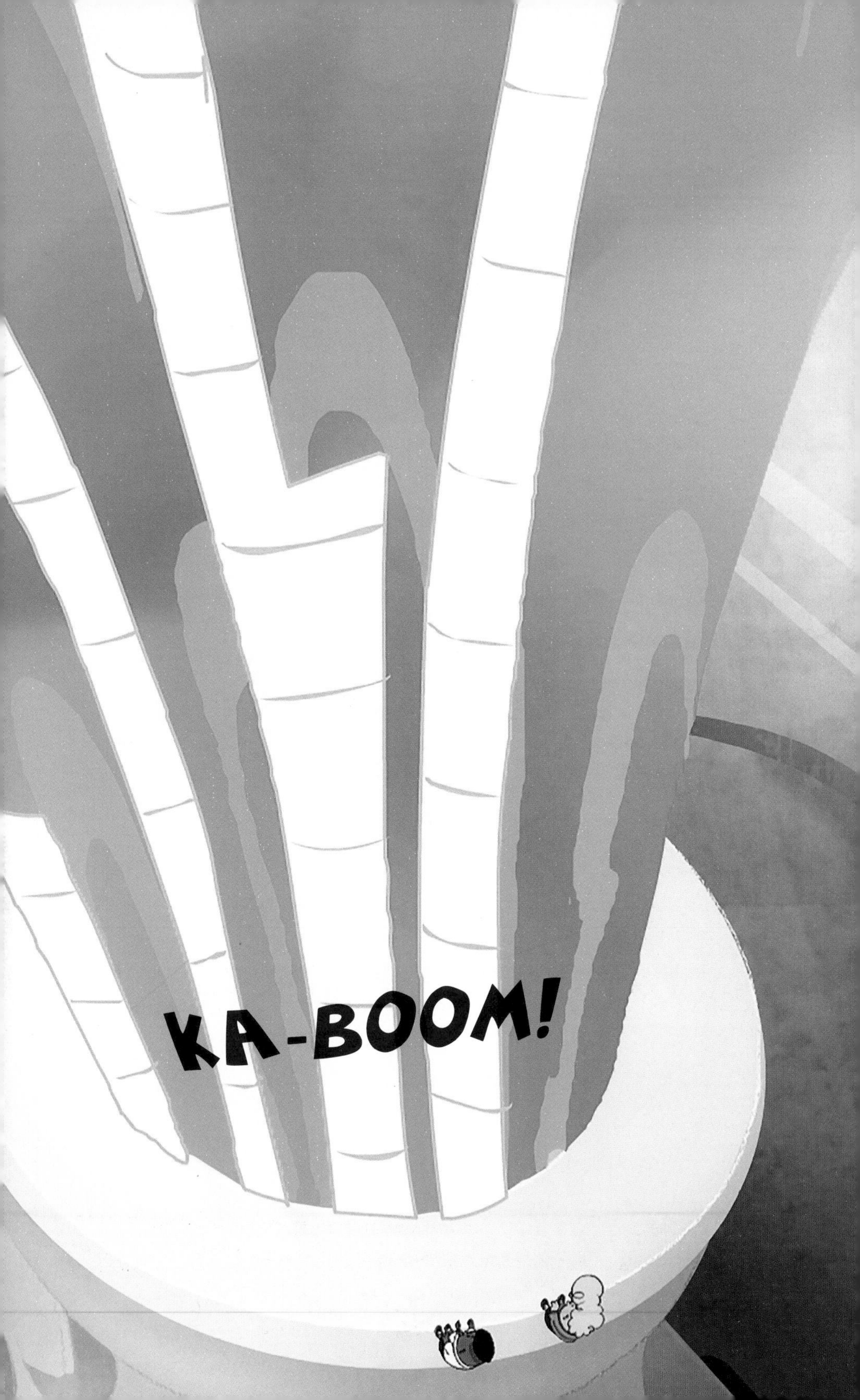
KA-BOOM!

CHAPTER 6

TO MAKE A SHORT STORY SHORTER

It did work.
Where am I? And what's that smell?

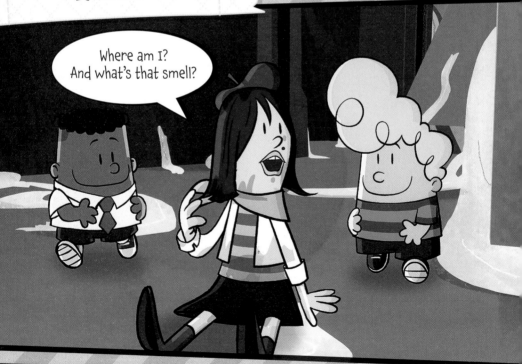

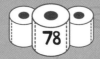

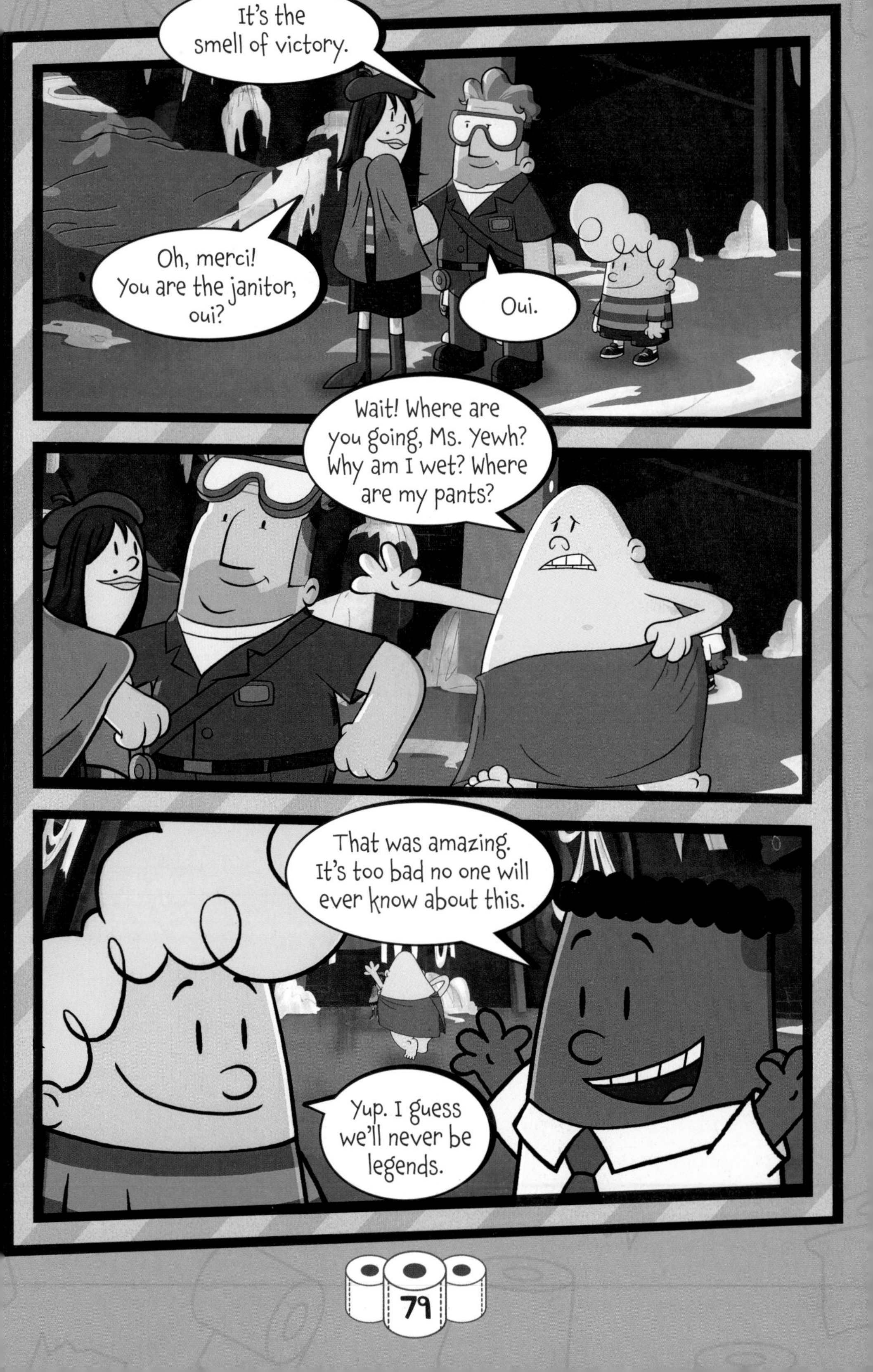
It's the smell of victory.
Oh, merci! You are the janitor, oui?
Oui.
Wait! Where are you going, Ms. Yewh? Why am I wet? Where are my pants?
That was amazing. It's too bad no one will ever know about this.
Yup. I guess we'll never be legends.

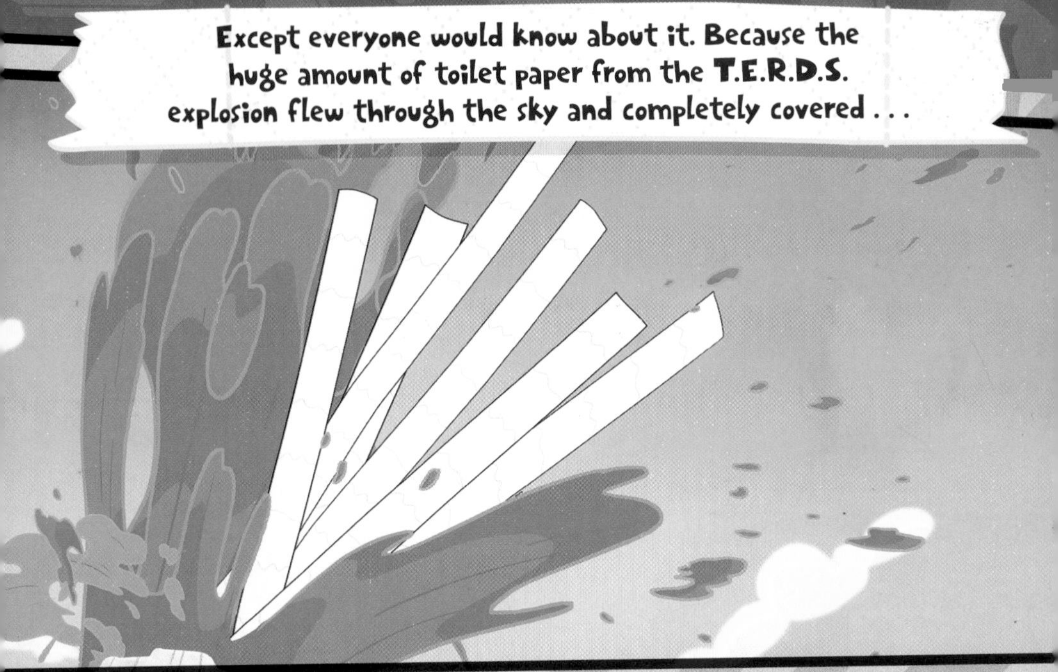
Except everyone would know about it. Because the huge amount of toilet paper from the T.E.R.D.S. explosion flew through the sky and completely covered . . .

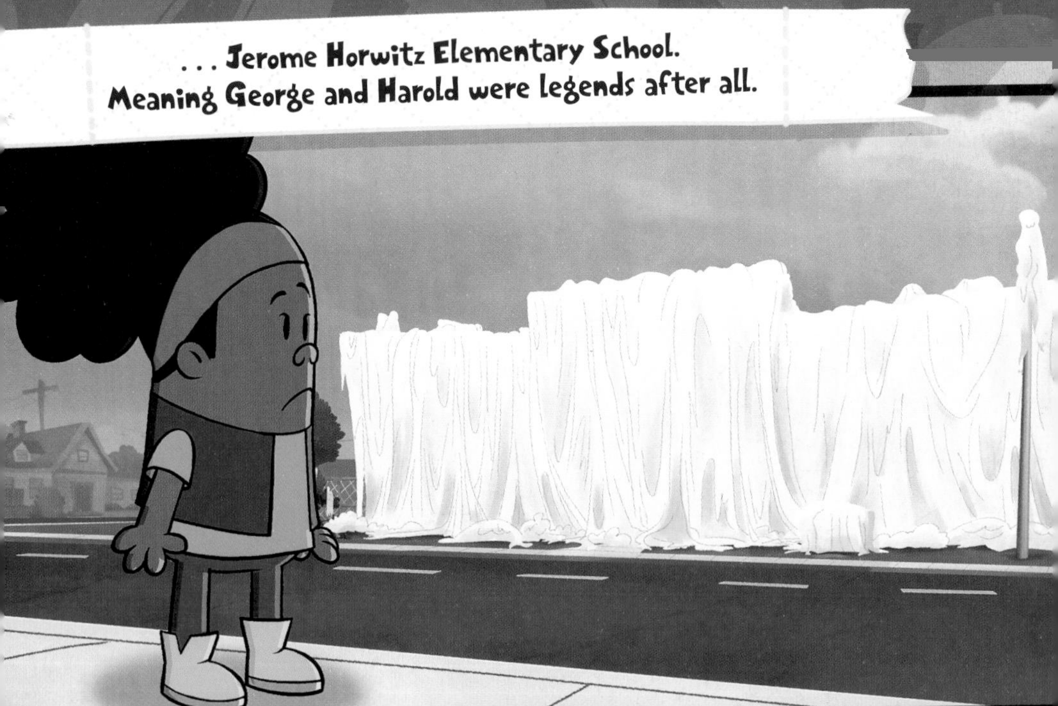
. . . Jerome Horwitz Elementary School. Meaning George and Harold were legends after all.